The Electric Telepath

www.kidsatrandomhouse.co.uk

Also by Jan Mark

A Can of Worms

Enough Is Too Much Already

They Do Things Differently There

Something in the Air

Useful Idiots

jan mark

The Electric Telepath

DEFINITIONS

THE ELECTRIC TELEPATH
A DEFINITIONS BOOK 0 099 43235 8

First published in Great Britain by Definitions,
an imprint of Random House Children's Books

This edition published 2005

1 3 5 7 9 10 8 6 4 2

Papers used by Random House Children's Books are natural, recyclable products made from wood grown in sustainable forests. The manufacturing processes conform to the environmental regulations of the country of origin.

Set in 11.5/14.5pt Caslon by
Falcon Oast Graphic Art Ltd.

Definitions are published by Random House Children's Books,
61–63 Uxbridge Road, London W5 5SA,
a division of The Random House Group Ltd,
in Australia by Random House Australia (Pty) Ltd,
20 Alfred Street, Milsons Point, Sydney, NSW 2061, Australia,
in New Zealand by Random House New Zealand Ltd,
18 Poland Road, Glenfield, Auckland 10, New Zealand,
and in South Africa by Random House (Pty) Ltd,
Endulini, 5A Jubilee Road, Parktown 2193, South Africa

THE RANDOM HOUSE GROUP Limited Reg. No. 954009
www.**kidsatrandomhouse**.co.uk

A CIP catalogue record for this book is available from the British Library.

Printed and bound in Great Britain by
Cox & Wyman Ltd, Reading, Berkshire

For Martha Westwater

One

'Now that's a fine figure of a woman,' Gunnings said, walking backwards to get a better view. 'I never could resist a well-turned ankle.'

The girl, who had unwisely caught his attention by elbowing him out of her way, flounced angrily and quickened her step. Elijah could see that she was dying to turn round and tell him to button his lip. He rather wished himself that Gunnings would button his lip. Gunnings could fool around all he liked at the town end of Station Road but down here, on the very slope of the railway bridge, they were uncomfortably close to Elijah's own territory.

'What's the matter? You don't *know* her, do you?' Gunnings could usually tell what Elijah was thinking. 'Not one of your Daughters of Sixtus, is it?'

'Sisters of Dorcas. Stow it, will you?'

Sooner or later Gunnings really would make one of his unfortunate remarks to someone from the chapel, a Sister of Dorcas even, and if Elijah were seen in his company there would be the Devil to pay later. Not that anyone would use that word, of course. Members of the Congregation of Mount Horeb spoke only of the Evil One, with lowered voices and in much the same tones as they mentioned drains.

Gunnings collided with a pram pushed by a scowling

nursemaid. Elijah, who before now had seen Gunnings go down on his knees in the street to apologize to aggrieved pedestrians, grabbed his elbow, turning him right-side round, and steered him onwards in spite of the nursemaid's full and frankly expressed opinion of people who were too tiddled to know which way they were going.

'She thinks you're drunk,' Elijah said.

'Intoxicated with your beauty, madam!' Gunnings called over his shoulder.

Gunnings always needed to let off steam after a day in school, especially on Fridays. The Congregation of Mount Horeb never let off steam; they had no steam to let off, emitting no more, Elijah considered, than a constant dribble of condensation. Without the fear of being seen by one of them he might have enjoyed the daily walk home in Gunning's frisky company, even if he dared not join in.

They had almost reached the summit of the bridge when Gunnings yelled, 'Loco on the right!' and broke into a run. Elijah took off after him. They were far too old to be racing trains but it was safer than chasing girls and they had been doing it for years. In fact, Elijah had started it after thinking innocently that it would be fun to stand in a pure cloud of cool white vapour as the train passed under the bridge and had found himself instead enveloped in hot and stinking sulphurous smoke.

They cleared the bridge with seconds to spare, narrowly missing a wagon that was turning out of the station approach. Gunnings continued to hurry.

'Can't hang about, off to London in the morning. Uncle Bertie's standing treat. No need to ask where you're going.'

Elijah jogged after him but Gunnings was headed to the right where the road branched, Elijah going straight on. Off to spend an hour with your guilty secret, I suppose.'

'It's not a guilty secret.'

'Well, you keep it pretty secret and you're as guilty as sin about it,' Gunnings said. 'I don't know why you don't tell your governor straight out. He can't shoot you.'

'I tried. I did tell him I needed to use the reading room. It's not my fault if he thinks it's the one in the Town Hall.'

'It's your fault he doesn't know it isn't. Pusillanimous, that's what you are.'

'What?'

'Pusillanimous. Good word, ain't it? I found it in Chapman's *Iliad*.'

'What's it mean?'

Gunnings had already crossed the road. 'Look it up in the dicker. See you on Monday!'

With a cheery wave he was round the corner and out of sight. Elijah trudged on up Trimley Road, towards his guilty secret.

Pusillanimous: proceeding from a want of courage. Elijah shoved the dictionary back on to its shelf and returned to his table. Gunnings was wrong, he did not want courage. 'Tell your governor,' Gunnings had said. Tell the Old Man? Oh, he could tell him all right. It was the subsequent arguments Elijah could not face. Arguing with his father was like wrestling with a feather bed.

Twin signs were screwed to the wall above the table and he saw them every time he raised his head.

SILENCE

NO TOBACCO NO SPITTING NO INK

Further along was a third, THOU GOD SEEST ME, a reminder that anyone who was tempted to spit or take out a bottle of ink would be under the eye of the Almighty even if the superintendent failed to notice.

Elijah would have preferred to be using ink but the Trimley Road Reading Room for the Advancement of the Working Man had banned it in the wake of some ancient mishap. A sprawling rusty stain darkened the boards in the middle of the floor as if someone had dashed down a cuttlefish that had burst on impact. Many of the older books were blotted and flecked; all were greasily thumbed and dog-eared. The superintendent was fighting a losing battle against smoke, fog, soot, gas fumes; at least he could take a stand over ink.

Elijah took out his pencil, opened his diary and made a note of the fact that had just struck him on seeing the date of that day's copy of the *Lembridge and District Intelligencer*, Friday 21 September. Tomorrow was the birthday of Michael Faraday. Were he yet living he would be 103, but Faraday was dead, James Clerk Maxwell was dead and so, too, now was Heinrich Hertz, on the first day of this year 1894. All his heroes had been taken and Faraday had gone first, but Elijah felt his loss most keenly. The great scientist had begun as a bookbinder's apprentice and Elijah seemed to see the hand of fate in that. *He* was a bookbinder's son, which might have put them on an equal footing, but Faraday's bookbinder had been a learned man who urged his apprentice to educate himself.

Elijah's bookbinder, his father, was Joseph Briggs, Town Councillor and Elder of the Congregation of Mount Horeb. From studying the great man's life Elijah knew that Faraday too had been chapel, an even smaller and more exclusive sect than the Congregation of Mount Horeb, but whatever it had been – strange, small, exclusive – it could never have forbidden him to *think*. Faraday had been encouraged to read the books he was binding. Collymore and Briggs Bindery was in the town centre, where profane novels and incendiary works of science were out of the reach of Joseph's corruptible offspring, which was why Elijah was sitting in the Trimley Road reading room. God might be watching him but Father wasn't.

Keeping the pencil poised to take down any other items of interest, he resumed his study of the *Scientific Digest*. He was supposed to be doing his homework, but homework had to be done in ink. Father regretfully allowed him to use a public reading room because it was understood that he needed certain works of reference that could not be kept at home, only Father was under the impression that the reading room was the one attached to the Free Library in the Town Hall. Since the Trimley Road establishment was a Church of England foundation the Old Man would never set foot in it and discover that, far from doing his homework, Elijah was reading material that would not be allowed into the house.

Very little material was allowed into the house that had not been approved by Headquarters in Halifax or by the chapel Elders in Cater Street. Father did not know that Elijah had been set on the path to temptation by a book so apparently harmless that it had not even been submitted for inspection: a family magazine from forty years ago bound up into an annual; hundreds of close-printed pages of hints on household management, recipes, crochet patterns, instructions on decorative leather-work, on making an aquarium, on teaching oneself to play the piano, interspersed with jokes, riddles, anecdotes; all hopelessly frivolous but not actively harmful. What had escaped Father's notice was a section at the back devoted to readers' questions. The questions themselves were not printed but someone had evidently written in asking how to make an electric friction machine. Elijah had not been able to believe his luck when he saw that.

As a member of the Modern side at school, he had abandoned Latin and Greek for mathematics, history and geography. Being in the Vth form allowed him access twice a week to a room laughingly referred to as 'the lab', one end assigned to chemistry – stinks – the other to what the *Scientific Digest* still called natural philosophy: physics.

There they could play about with bar magnets and stroke moulting cat skins with carbon rods, and fiddle with the Wimshurst machine, collecting static electricity in Leyden jars. It was an hour of frustration for Elijah. Physics, surely, was the key to the future, but entering the lab was like unlocking a door to the past. The electricity they produced was antique electricity; its time was over. Where were the electromagnetic waves of Heinrich Hertz, where were the motors? What of the power stations –

Ferranti's in Deptford, Edison's hydroelectric plant in America? What were they supposed to do with their schoolboy sparks and shocks? Why were they not following where Faraday and Maxwell and Hertz had led?

But he knew that it was not enough to follow; a true disciple had to go back and begin where they had begun. 'Every student of science should be an antiquary of his subject,' Maxwell himself had written. An antiquary – an historian. Elijah, aching to carry on where the three heroes had left off, nevertheless followed Maxwell's advice and was trying to become an historian of his subject. Using the diagram and instructions in the *Family Friend*, he and Gunnings had managed to get a friction machine up and running, using an old bottle instead of a glass cylinder. Flush with this success, they had assembled a wet-cell battery and a galvanometer, but they had no means of using the electricity they produced and could only collect it in Leyden jars as they did at school. Elijah had provided most of the components with the aid of a chemist in the High Street, but everything had to be kept at Gunning's place. There was no question of taking it home to Ryecart Road and leaving it where Father would see it. If he hid it in the room he shared with his brother Ezra, Ezra would find it, which was much the same as Father finding it. Ezra believed in spreading glad tidings.

Observing the injunction for silence, the clock on the wall clicked and whirred without striking – six o'clock. Most working men being still at work, he had the place to himself; he could risk another fifteen minutes before he headed home, but he ought just to look at his schoolwork

– he still hadn't done that tracing from Gardiner's *Atlas of English History*. Then he remembered that he had mislaid the book. It was a school copy, too, and if it did not turn up before Monday he would catch it from Mr Ballard, who behaved as though the cost of every book, every inkwell, every pen nib, had come out of his own pocket.

It must be at home. If it really were lost he would have to fork out for a new one and he resented the thought of that in his last year at school. He returned to the limp greasy pages of the *Scientific Digest*. It was better than nothing, but the editor's definition of scientific was indiscriminate, to put it mildly. The *Digest* was a forum for guesswork. Anyone with a bright idea found house room in its pages: spirit voices, influencing rays, spirit photographs, therapeutic machines, telepathy - 'theoretically the next stage in the evolution of language' – waves that could pass through walls—

No, that was not guesswork, it was a serious proposition from a serious scientist, the chemist William Crookes, written only a couple of years ago:

> Rays of light will not pass through a wall nor, as we know only too well, through a London fog, but the electrical vibrations of a yard or more in wave-length . . . will easily pierce mediums which to them will be transparent . . . telegraphy without wires . . . posts, cables . . . mutual receptivity . . .

Telegraphy without wires: these were the Hertzian waves he had been reading about in the *Electrician* only recently, produced by discharging an electromagnetic coil across a gap between terminals. Two people with the right apparatus could send signals to each other along the waves, signals that would pass through walls, window-panes – what sort of signals? Morse code, according to Crookes.

Elijah knew about this. Oliver Lodge, another hero, still living, had only recently done it. Why should he not make a Hertzian apparatus for himself? He had made electro-magnets, winding the coils as Faraday had done, religiously adhering to the same specifications, and look at what Faraday had started.

It was already growing dark when he left the reading room and stepped into the dank bustle of Trimley Road. The streetlamps were lit; gas, of course. No chance here of seeing what Faraday had started, no electric lighting anywhere in the Trident or even in central Lembridge. Shop windows were gas lit and so were the offices of Cadell and Roper, Estate Agents, Auctioneers, next to the reading room. No one had ever met Cadell, but Roper lived at the far end of Elijah's own street. He could be seen now, from the pavement, through the open door of his inner office, ostentatiously speaking into a telephone.

His two windows were plate glass, one displaying pictures of desirable properties to let or for sale. These were situated well away from Trimley Road, on Holloway Hill. The second contained nothing but a large map with a gilded arrow pointing to the very spot where Elijah stood envying Mr Roper's telephone. *Belvedere*, it announced in

Gothic lettering along the top. He knew what that meant – beautiful view. Oh, had they only but known . . .

Coming in at the left of the map was Station Road, which branched into three after crossing the railway. However estate agents and builders chose to describe it, the area was known for what it looked like, a trident. Trimley Road was the middle prong, Holloway Hill bounded it on the north side, Milton Road to the south. Thirty years ago the whole area south-east of the railway had been a grassy hillside with small farms, garden plots, a few cottages dotted along cart tracks, and the brick fields. Milton Road had been the main thoroughfare out of Lembridge, Trimley Road a lane, Hollow Way a footpath over the hill. The history of its ongoing transformation was recorded on Roper's map. From the outset its claims to being a beautiful view had been severely compromised by the iron foundry and the gasworks, conveniently close to the marshalling yards. Houses had sprung up along Trimley Road, then shops. Holloway Hill had been macadamized; streets crept between the three main roads like webs between fingers. The two longest of these were at the eastern end of the prongs. Elijah lived in Ryecart Road. On Cater Street stood the chapel of the Congregation of Mount Horeb.

They were modest streets lined with modest houses. Bigger houses, of the kind advertised in Roper's window, were built along Milton Road and Holloway Hill in the first surge of enthusiasm for the dream of Belvedere, an elegant suburb where refined persons might live in semi-rural retreat from town. It had not worked out quite like that. Every time Roper made a sale his clerk removed the map and shaded in the area that was about to be built on. In the three years that Elijah had been walking home from school up Trimley Road he had watched the map become a triangular mosaic of black and white.

Now the black patches outnumbered the white as the buildings crept ever eastwards along the prongs, across the webs. Any refined persons who had bought properties at the western end of Milton Road and the eastern end of Holloway Hill were out on the fringes of the Trident, at a safe distance from what they perceived to be its seething sinful heart. From that safe distance they had written to the *Intelligencer* pointing out that although there were shops on every corner of Belvedere, as they persisted in calling it, and a public house in every street (of the lowest kind, naturally), there was no place of worship in the whole Godless area. With the nearest parish church in Trimley village, the suburb was in urgent need of salvation. Who should have been the first to come riding to the rescue but the Congregation of Mount Horeb. Their chapel was on Roper's map, a narrow black rectangle occupying a whole plot in Cater Street.

Elijah left the lighted shops behind and hurried through the dark place where the new Anglican church was at last rising from its foundations on the right and the workhouse loomed on the left, past the allotment gardens at the end of Cater Street and the tram depot, and on to Ryecart Road. It was beginning to rain. The tramlines shone among the setts like curving brush strokes of wet paint.

What a difference electric light would make, he

thought, rounding the corner. This stretch of Ryecart Road was nearly half a mile long and between him and the other end were ten gas lamps, five on each side. Most housewives had drawn their curtains, a few hallways were lit. Few houses at this end had hallways. The road receded dimly before him, the only bright patch the open gates of Morrell's forge and that was closing for the night, the last horse shod, the fire damped down.

The other pair of double gates on the far side of the road, where the Aubrey clan had their scrap yard. Jack Morrell kept the entrance to his smithy hospitably open, roaring out greetings to anyone who passed on heady waves of singed hoof, glowing coals, hot iron. The Aubreys' gates were always shut except when William Senior or William Junior drove their cart out into the road, but they could be heard at all hours of the day and most of the night, even from the Briggses' house, several doors down and on the opposite side.

The male Aubreys – there were also a grandfather, William the First – seemed to exist in a state of armed confrontation. From over the gates came fusillades of oaths and the sound of missiles striking breakable targets. A harridan of uncertain age, presumably married to one of the Williams, chimed in with a descant of unintelligible shrieks. It must have been the sight and sound of the Aubreys, Elijah thought, that had alarmed the good Christians of Belvedere into demanding places of worship for the infidels of the Trident, which made it all the stranger that on occasional Sundays, and even more occasional Wednesday evenings, Williams Senior and

Junior presented themselves at the Cater Street chapel. Sometimes accompanied by William the First or the ambiguous Mrs Aubrey, they would sit in a glowering clump in the foremost pew, confronting the twelve Elders, who beamed benevolently upon them like the sun on thunderclouds.

Elijah paused on his doorstep and looked along the road at the double gates with the legend WM AUBREY AND SON RAGS BONES OLD IRON RABBIT SKINS painted in a crescent of tall white capitals. It was unnervingly silent except for the crackle of flames which leaped ten feet into the air above the gates. Perhaps they had finally all killed each other, he thought briefly, and let himself into the hall, followed by a strong smell of burning India rubber. It made a change from the sickening gusts of rabbit-skin glue, the boiling up of which was an Aubrey sideline.

The Briggs house had no front garden but a paved area where Elder Briggs kept the chapel handcart chained to the boot scraper and Elijah's sister Agnes had raised a plant of uncertain species in a pot by the steps. Defeated by gas fumes, coal smoke and rabbit-skin glue, it put out fewer leaves each spring, shedding them at the first sign of autumn, and autumn came early to the doorstep. The plant was already naked. Only the aspidistra on the parlour windowsill flourished in its green-glazed pot, leaves akimbo, impervious to gas and taking on all comers.

Elijah hunt up his cap and jacket, slung his satchel at the foot of the stairs and went along the twilit hall, where the gas jet, turned down to its lowest, simmered under a green glass shade. We had given up arguing that if they must economize on gas wouldn't it be more efficient to have white shades or even clear glass? Apparently not. The mottled green shades had been there when Elder and Mrs Briggs had moved into the house and there they must remain, as though God had ordained it in the Book of Leviticus, proof of His immutable word.

O Faraday! O Edison! If only they could have electric light.

Two

'I am forbidding nothing,' said Elder Briggs, looming mildly from behind the teapot where it stood in the centre of the table. 'It is not my place to forbid. There is only One who can direct the path of a human life—'

'Then Dad, surely—'

'But by that same token I am not the one from whom to seek permission or even guidance. Watch and pray. Listen for the still small voice. It was not for nothing that you were named Elijah.'

'How long must I listen?'

'For as long as is needful,' his father said.

Elijah, head bent, fixed his eyes on the plate in front of him, counting breadcrumbs. How long did *you* listen? He demanded silently, aiming his thought across the teapot at the Old Man. How long was it before the still small voice told you to go forth and become a bookbinder? What did you *want* to be?

'Do not think that I don't understand,' Elder Briggs said. 'At your age I was still learning to subdue my will. My father wished me to follow him into the law, and I would have been happy to obey, but there was One to whom I owed obedience even before my own parent.'

Elijah kept his eyes on the breadcrumbs. It was uncanny, the way the Old Man so often seemed to know what he was thinking. On the other hand, hadn't he in a sense asked the question that his father was even now long-windedly answering?

'I wrestled with my desire to please my father and to please myself, and the struggle seemed unavailing, and then at last, when I had ceased to struggle, I heard the still small voice. And when I told my parents we knew that this was the path that I must follow.'

He was omitting the part where Grandfather, incensed by Dad's decision, had thrown him out of the house and cut him out of his will. Grandfather had not belonged to the Congregation of Mount Horeb.

It would be so easy, Elijah thought, to come skipping down to breakfast one morning with a gladsome face, and cry to the family, 'Last night I heard the still small voice. God has told me to stay at school for another two years and then go to university to study physics.'

Would he be able to seem gladsome enough or would his guilty falsehood shine malignantly like a corpse light through his frank and open countenance? He was more likely to be believed if he burst in on them crying, 'The Lord has told me to go down to the railway station and get a job in the ticket office where I can spread the word of the still small voice to people who are trying to catch trains.'

His father knew of his passion to study physics, to follow the example of his hero Michael Faraday, the bookbinder's apprentice. Wasn't it divine intervention, if not the hand of Fate, that had arranged for the defecting law student to be employed by Collymore the Horebite bookbinder, who had taken Father into his firm for the sake of the Congregation and had ended up making him a partner? Father was not even insisting that he became a bookbinder himself. It wasn't as though he begrudged Elijah his upkeep while he studied, as an apprentice, as a student; he grudged him nothing. Most of the neighbourhood boys of his age were already earning. Father would happily support him for the rest of his life so long as he were dedicated to the Congregation of Mount Horeb, spreading the word of the Lord through the still small voice.

And considering how still and small it seemed to be it wielded a disproportionate power over their lives. Two years after Mother died, giving birth to Ezra, Elder Briggs had formed an attachment to Susannah Weller of Trimley. Elijah and his brother and sisters, who were fond of Susannah, had urged him vocally and in their prayers, but Elder Briggs and Miss Weller had waited for the still small voice.

After a further two years nothing had been said to Father, but a voice of some sort had drawn Miss Weller's attention to a farmer from Milton way, and Elijah's elder sister Agnes had resigned herself to managing the household, as she had been doing since Mother died.

'And did the still small voice speak to you?' Elijah had asked her once, in a moment of exasperation. 'Were you told to stay at home and look after the rest of us instead of getting married?'

Agnes had been deeply shocked. She would be the first to see through any lie Elijah tried to tell them. She suspected that he was not as truly submissive as he had to appear to be. Abigail and Ezra, six and eight years younger than he was, trotted about so piously that he wanted to kick them, particularly Ezra. If Ezra were to be believed, the still small voice spoke to him so often that he was practically on nodding terms with it. Abigail believed him, the little tick, and burdened herself with the sin of envy because she was too honest to claim that it had spoken to her.

Elder Briggs folded his hands and raised his eyes to the ceiling. 'Imbue us, o Lord, with gratitude for this thy bounty, in our hearts and minds. Amen.'

The family's amens echoed the Old Man's voice as he stood up.

'Another meeting, Father?' Agnes said.

'The Board of the Asylum for Unfortunates,' Elder Briggs said. 'I shall not be late.'

Unfortunates, Elijah had worked out, were people whose families found them embarrassing to the point where they would do anything to get them off the premises. They had Weaknesses: for drink, laudanum, members of the opposite sex – or even the same sex, Elijah had deduced, reading between the lines of the minutes books. The still small voice did not reach them. Stentor himself with Edison's megaphone would not reach them.

'Elijah, go to your room for an hour and *listen*,' his father said, stepping into the hall. Abigail ran after him to fetch his coat and muffler for the three-hundred-yard journey to the chapel of Mount Horeb in Cater Street. The words were not spoken unkindly. Elijah was not being banished, sent upstairs in disgrace like a naughty child. His father sincerely wished him to be happy, would accept it if the still small voice truly directed him to go forth and be a scientist; but, convinced of an afterlife that would last for Eternity, could not see that a delay of a few months, or a few years, or possibly a couple of decades, could make very much difference. And in any case, he could see little chance of its happening. The Congregation of Mount Horeb was wary of science. Obviously their God was of the same mind.

Elijah went up to his room. At the chapel whole evenings might be spent kneeling, in silence, while the brethren and sisters waited to hear the still small voice. He drew the line at that in private and sat at his desk, head in hands, staring out of the uncurtained window over the dark garden.

His room faced the backs of the houses in Cater Street, and in a distant window he saw a candle burning. In a room like his someone else, perhaps another Horebite, was sitting waiting. And time was passing, it was hurtling by. Never mind Eternity, there would be no science in heaven. How could he bear to wait any longer while his classmates left school and went to work, or went to university, *did* something, anything, and he was left behind listening, for the voice that never spoke.

It wasn't that he did not believe; he did. What he could not believe was that he, Elijah Vernon Briggs, had been put on earth solely to convey the doctrine of the Congregation of Mount Horeb to the people who lived in the Trident, trudging from door to door to beseech the doubtful, the derisive, the downright hostile, to listen for what he did not hear himself.

Michael Faraday had not been to university but he had managed to get a job assisting Sir Humphry Davy, and after that there had been no stopping him. There were no new Humphry Davys in Lembridge, but there must be a way to get started without waiting for the still small voice. Faraday's discoveries were at last bearing fruit: electric light, electric motors, the electric telegraph, the telephone. Continents could communicate with each other via the undersea cables to America and Europe; one day they might even be able to do it on the telephone; and now there were waves that might carry sound, not along wires but invisibly, through the air, the ones he had been reading about in the *Scientific Digest*. Hertz's apparatus seemed to be simple enough, anyone could make it. There was no reason at all why he should not make it himself, but where would he keep it?

He gazed round the room. He had to share it with Ezra and Ezra could be relied upon to poke about and ask questions in his pious, penetrating treble. There was nothing still or small about Ezra's voice. 'Oh, 'lijah, whatever can this be?' That had been when he discovered the bar magnet cylinder. It was fear of Ezra's quivering antennae that had forced Elijah to construct and keep the friction machine and the other equipment at Gunning's place. If he made an induction coil and Ezra found it, the whole house would know, the whole street would know, and then Father would be perturbed. It was his only expression of displeasure. Other people's parents were vexed, annoyed; they waxed wroth. Father would admit to nothing more than being perturbed, a still small voice of disquiet. He would be perturbed because it would seem to him that Elijah was jumping the gun, making preparations for a life of science to which he had not been and might not be called, and there would be more admonitions to listen for the SSV.

Elijah did not call it the SSV in public. The Congregation of Mount Horeb would be shocked to hear the central tenet of their faith reduced to a set of initials.

The light in the distant window rose and receded. Someone had picked up the candle and left the room. Elijah stared into the darkness. Was someone out there, unseen, looking in at him? He listened. He really did listen. *Speak to me. Thy servant heareth.*

He tried to empty his mind, to think of nothing, so that if the SSV should speak, nothing would interfere. The clock in the hall below struck eight, followed by the church clock in town. Time was passing, the hour was more than up—

Into his head came the thought, *Gunnings has got my Gardiner's Atlas.*

This was not, he had to admit, likely to be the still small voice of God, but no matter who had sent the message he was glad to get it. He had been searching for the book for days, convinced that he must have put it down carelessly somewhere, perhaps at school, perhaps – please, God, no – on the tram.

He would not have forgotten lending the book to Gunnings – where had the thought come from? It was several hours since he had remembered its loss in the

Trimley Road reading room and he had not been thinking about it when the words came into his head.

How had they come into his head? He had not heard anything; the thought was suddenly there. Wasn't that how the SSV was supposed to communicate, not in the blinding flash of light that had felled St Paul on the road to Damascus, but in silence? Gunnings lived only a few minutes' walk away on the far side of Milton Road, outside the Trident. Ought he to go round now and find out? No – Gunnings was off on some jaunt this weekend and anyway, Father was still at the chapel – committee meetings rarely ended before nine. Because of the suppose depravity of the neighbourhood the Old Man did not care to have Agnes and the children alone in the house after dark if it could be avoided. Elijah thought it must be the number of public houses that made Christians fear for public morals, but at the rate things were going there would soon be more chapels than pubs. An honest artisan, slaking his thirst after a hard day at the foundry or the sawmill, could not step out of his local without being assailed by enquiries about the state of his soul. At least the Horebites left all that to the SSV.

The nearest pub was a goodish step down the street and mainly used by men from the brickworks who, if they were inclined to terrorize women and children, went home and terrorized their own. But if Elijah went out to see Gunnings he would be sure to run into a brother Horebite, who would mention it to Father, concerned that Elijah was putting his immortal soul at risk upon the sinful streets of the Trident after dark. And then there was

Ezra, who'd be certain to let slip something of his own when Father returned.

'Oh, Papa, we were so afraid alone here tonight, but we prayed earnestly to God to watch over us and protect Elijah *while he was out*.'

Ezra must die, he thought viciously, and pulled himself up short. Suppose thoughts *could* be transmitted; he might find himself a fratricide. After all, Father had picked up what he had been thinking at tea time, across the table, and he certainly hadn't been transmitting then, far from it. He had wanted to keep his thoughts to himself. How would he feel if he went down now and found Ezra stretched out lifeless in the kitchen with Agnes wringing her hands and Abigail awash with tears over the tiny corpse?

He turned down the gas and went downstairs. The parlour door was closed as it always was unless they were entertaining visitors. Father's study was empty of course, but from the kitchen he could hear Ezra's reedy recitation of a psalm.

He had not slain his brother, he'd never really thought he had, but there were known to be societies in far-flung parts of Empire where witch-doctors could slay with a thought. People *did* believe, even now, in ill-wishing. There might be something in it – that message about the atlas must have come from somewhere.

His real fear had been that he had left the book on the tram, not only because it might not have been handed in but because none of them was supposed to take the tram except in special circumstances – the second coming, perhaps.

'Before making an expenditure,' ran the Mount Horeb thoughts for guidance in the conduct of everyday life, 'ask yourself, "Is this expenditure necessary?" Then ask yourself how you would define "necessary". Do you in fact mean desirable? Convenient? Pleasurable? If you can agree with yourself that the expenditure is indeed needful, make it. If there remains any lingering doubt, forgo the expenditure and make an equivalent contribution to the mission treasury for the relief of want in others.'

Downstairs on the kitchen mantelpiece was what the family, with heavy Horebite humour, called the Necessary Jar. It had once held pickles. Whenever one of them decided that an expenditure was no more than desirable, convenient or downright pleasurable, the equivalent contribution was dropped into the Necessary Jar. Once a week Father conveyed the money to the chapel, where it was diverted into one of the relief funds. Elijah had once imagined that at the back of the chapel there must be an enormous Necessary Jar, like those in a chemist's window, red, purple, green, filled with shining coins. He still recalled his disappointment when he was first shown the cash boxes, locked and labelled and stored prosaically in a safe.

He genuinely approved of the scheme, but he had taken the tram home from school that day because he was late and it was raining and he could not see why he must examine his conscience about spending a halfpenny which might otherwise find its way into the pocket of a Private Soldier Lately Discharged from Her Majesty's Service who would spend it very sensibly on unnecessary beer.

* * *

There was no need to approach Gunnings. As Elijah went into the Vth form room on Monday morning, Gunnings rose from his desk with a book in his hand.

'Hey, Briggs, weren't you looking for this?'

The book was Gardiner's *Atlas of English History*.

'What are you doing with it?' Elijah could hardly believe what he was seeing and hearing. 'I didn't lend it to you.'

'No need to take it like that.' Gunnings looked hurt. 'I didn't steal the thing. Must have picked it up by accident with my own stuff. Suddenly spotted it on Friday night. Here's a go, I thought, I've got two Gardiners, they must be multiplying.'

'When?' Elijah said. How *could* he have known?

'When did they multiply? I don't know. Put them back and we might have four by this evening – spontaneous fission— Oh, I see. When did I pinch it? Must have been *last* Monday, after history.'

'I meant, when did you discover you had it?'

'I told you, Friday night – clearing out my satchel. There was a sandwich squashed away at the bottom – now, that *was* breeding. A splendid crop of *mucor*. I'll give it to the Lower Fourth for their nature table.'

'Can you remember *exactly* when?'

'Were you frantic about it? Gosh, I'm sorry. I'd have brought it round on Saturday but we were off to London at dawn.'

'No, I wasn't frantic,' Elijah said, 'but something really rum happened on Friday night. I suddenly had this thought: Gunnings has got my Gardiner's atlas. I was coming to ask you just now when you waved it in my face.'

'Really? What a coincidence. But how could you have thought that. You didn't know – *I* didn't know.'

'That's what's rum. I didn't know – but I *did* think it.'

'It was definitely after supper . . .' Gunnings appeared to go into a trance. 'I was in my room . . . when did you get the thought?'

'Eight o'clock. When did you think it?'

'It couldn't have been later than ten past because I was downstairs when old Harboard came round to see Dad – you must have been reading my mind.'

'Telepathy,' Elijah said.

'Thought reading. Parlour trick, ain't it? I say, that's an idea though. We could get up an act, like illusionists do, go on the halls.'

Elijah gathered that Gunnings's London jaunt had included a visit to an illusionist's act. It was not a visit he was ever likely to make and he did not even bother to wonder what his father would say to the suggestion that his elder son might earn his living as a music-hall turn. Perturbation wouldn't come into it.

'"Telepathy is theoretically the next stage in the evolutions of language."' He was quoting from the *Scientific Digest*. Evolutionary theory of any kind was shunned by the Congregation of Mount Horeb. Elijah had read *The Origin of Species* and *The Descent of Man* in the Town Hall library, and he thought that Darwin had presented a pretty unarguable case. The Horebites believed that Archbishop Ussher had been correct in dating the Creation of the world to 4004 BC and that the fossils in the town museum had been created at the same time – living creatures that had perished in the Flood.

Elijah kept his opinions to himself. The only book at home on the subject was a slim self-satisfied volume, the author of which, while trying to appear scientifically detached, was evidently aghast at the suggestion that man, made in God's image, might share a common ancestor with a jellyfish.

'Evolution? You don't say.' Gunnings grinned. 'Well, it might be. It wasn't a trick last night, was it? At exactly the moment I discovered I had your Gardiner, the thought communicated itself to you. How?'

'It might not have been exact—'

'Near enough. Now, as you said, you *couldn't* have known I had it.'

'Ah, but suppose I'd known before you did. Suppose you hadn't been excavating for that sandwich? Then I'd have swanned in this morning and said, 'Gunnings, you rotter, you've got my Gardiner,' and you'd have denied it.'

'Yes, but that's not what happened.' Outside in the playground the bell was ringing. The little boys from the lower forms began to swarm. 'Look,' Gunnings said, 'are you game for an experiment? We'll fix a time and take it in turns to transmit a thought.'

'What, across the form room? Ah, now, if one of us had a crib he could tell the other one the answers.'

'I didn't mean using it to cheat,' Gunnings said. 'That would be an abuse of – of – of whatever it is. Don't you lot get smitten with ten plagues for thinking of things like that? You shock me, Briggs. Hey! I wonder if we can get thoughts from the future – Derby winners.'

'We can't do it in school, there'd be too many other thoughts getting in the way.' Elijah was vaguely dismayed by Gunnings's enthusiasm for a phenomenon that had left him only mildly intrigued – and so relieved to know where his atlas had got to. But there was no stopping Gunnings now.

'Let's agree on a time this evening and do it properly. The next stage in the evolution of language . . . Tell you what, Briggs, we could be on to something.'

Three

Elder Briggs was not aware that his son and Reginald Gunnings were friends. He knew that they must associate at school since they were in the same form, but any idea of friendship would have perturbed him severely. The Gunnings family were known to be freethinkers, which to the Congregation of Mount Horeb was tantamount to being Anarchists or even Nihilists. Their church-going was erratic, the family did not descend in a body upon St Asaph's in town every Sunday, or on any other place of worship.

Reginald did not let on to Elijah what his father thought of the Horebites, but Elijah knew, without recourse to thought reading. Both fathers would, for very different reasons, have objected to the experiment in telepathy, Dr Gunnings because he thought it was a sell, fit only for illusionists, Elder Briggs because he believed that there was only one voice that anyone ought to be listening for and also because he would have preferred it if Elijah's friends were drawn solely from the Congregation of Mount Horeb. Horebites should consort only with other Horebites, marry other Horebites and raise infant Horebites to keep the faith alight.

They were not meeting with any noticeable success. Few of the Congregation were under thirty and four of those were the Briggses. The Sisters of Dorcas, female arm of the Elders, were mainly married or past child-bearing age and the Elders themselves were, in the main, elderly. What was it about the Horebites that turned people's thoughts from procreation? The Wesleyans multiplied like rabbits; they even had their own school.

But when a young Horebite's fancy turned to thoughts of love, there were few to choose from. Elijah personally knew no girls of his own age in the Congregation. Agnes, at eighteen, was the nearest, but only the Pharaohs of Egypt married their own sisters. He thought of the likely response if he made a joke to Agnes about that. Perhaps it was the fear that they might die out that made proselytizing part of the Congregation's duty. In a cupboard at the back of the chapel were the minutes books of various committees: for the Relief of the Poor; for the Relief of Widows and Orphans of those Fallen in the Service of Her Majesty Overseas; for the Redemption of Fallen Women; the Asylum for Unfortunates; the League of Abstinence . . .

Elijah had discovered, after an embarrassing confusion, that there was more than one way of falling, and that fallen women were not in the same plight as fallen warriors, but the Horebites extended the open hand of charity to all. It was understood, however, that in return for relief and assistance, the relieved and assisted should keep an ear open for the still small voice. Aid was never withheld, but Elijah, unlike his innocent and charitable parent, suspected that it was the Necessary Jar that kept them in line. The still small voice was as domineering in its way as the hell-fire threats that the Horebites eschewed. It did not threaten, it nagged.

However, it was his duty, three evenings a week and on Saturdays, to visit those who had in a moment of fervour, or weakness, or exasperation, undertaken to listen. He loathed every moment of these visits. The needy tolerated them because often it was only the Horebites and the Jar that stood between them and destitution or the workhouse, but the Congregation was, on a larger scale, equally needy. The Necessary Jar had to be topped up on a regular basis. In matters of the spirit the Horebites welcomed everyone, rich and poor, but the rich were thin on the ground in the Trident and the ones on Milton Road and Holloway Hill, being of the St Asaph's persuasion, barely pretended to tolerate Elijah when he appeared on their doorsteps enquiring after the state of their souls and imploring them to listen for the still small voice. In any case, he rarely got beyond the servant who answered the door.

When he had settled on a particular time with Gunnings for the experiment in thought transference, he had forgotten that he was scheduled to be out and about in the Trident, annoying the neighbours.

They had agreed that the hour should be 6.30. This time Elijah would be sending the message, Gunnings receiving it. Gunnings would be at home now, sitting in silence in his room, the room he had to share with no one else, concentrating, listening. Elijah had imagined that he would be in his own room with Ezra temporarily out of the way because it was understood that Elijah must have peace and quiet for his homework. Instead, Elijah was out in the noisome dark of Union Street, west of the workhouse, east of the gasworks, waiting in the rain for the distant chimes of St Asaph's to mark the half hour.

When he heard the first notes of the first quarter he stood still in the mouth of an alleyway, out of range of any passing policeman, who would certainly approach and ask what he was doing, or preparing to do, with good reason. He closed his eyes, clasped his hands as though praying, and began to transmit.

He had given a lot of thought to the content of the message; there must be no leeway for guesswork. He was sure that Gunnings would be expecting him to transmit a line of a hymn, a verse from the Bible. He had rejected several ideas before he came up with the notice that he passed daily in the window of Elkington's cash chemists: PURE, PALE COD LIVER OIL, IMPORTED DIRECT FROM NEWFOUNDLAND, AS FREE FROM DISAGREEABLE TASTE AND ODOUR AS IT IS POSSIBLE TO BE OBTAINED.

He knew it by heart and rehearsed it in silence, slowly, a dozen times. It contained enough key words for the two of them to be certain that either the transmission had worked or it had been a total failure: 'cod', 'Newfoundland', 'pure', 'pale', 'taste', 'odour'. If Gunnings received any of those they might really be on to something. If he reported 'haddock' or 'Nova Scotia' they might be encouraged. If, however, he were left with a vague impression of cocoa or Arabia Deserta they would have to try again under more favourable conditions, or admit that there was nothing in it. Elijah personally doubted that there was anything in it. He was already wishing that he had said nothing to Gunnings; he could imagine what the

Congregation would have to say on the subject. Still, an experiment and its results had to be repeated to be called a success. If they failed he could forget about it, but he owed it to Gunnings to try, although he had spent the afternoon in the lab trying to transmit to Gunnings, in Roman history, 'The square on the hypotenuse of a right-angled triangle is equal to the sum of the squares on the two adjacent sides.' Gunnings did not appear to have noticed.

He transmitted once more, for luck – something which, as a Horebite, he did not officially believe in – slipped out of the alley and turned his steps towards Holloway Hill. The anticipated policeman did not pass until he was at a safe distance from the alley's mouth, walking his beat with purposeful tread in the rain that slicked his mackintosh cape, recognizing Elijah and greeting him with an affable, 'Good evening,' instead of a suspicious, 'What's all this then?'

Policemen, on the whole, approved of the Horebites. They saw them as a calming influence, and most of the local force knew Elijah by sight from their frequent calls on the Aubreys. Elijah himself dreaded having to call on the Aubreys but they were not on his list tonight. His final port of call was the home of Mrs Gilstrap at The Vista, on Holloway Hill.

Mrs Gilstrap, widow of the late Captain Frederick Gilstrap, lived in the last house on Holloway Hill, on the north side, looking down over the Trident. It would not be the last for long. Roper's map showed a row of lightly shaded rectangles stretching beyond it, and pairs of semi-detached villas were going up on the south side. The shoulder of the hill shielded them from the gasworks.

Elijah could not fathom how Mrs Gilstrap had come to be involved with the Congregation of Mount Horeb. He could understand that in the past some wandering Horebite had knocked on the door soliciting funds for the Necessary Jar. Moneyed people, happy to be associated with good works, would fork out – paying us to go away, Elijah thought grimly – but Mrs Gilstrap had, in addition, graciously consented to take the chair on one or two committees although she had not yet appeared in chapel, and was unlikely to. She was a church-goer, which in the view of the Congregation was equivalent to being a benighted heathen. She had not heard the still small voice. On the other hand, her contributions kept her pet committees afloat.

Elijah wished that she too would pay him to stay away. Mrs Gilstrap was a nice enough woman, if vague and ill at ease in his company. Had he been able to corner her on her own they might have managed half an hour's spiritual conversation, but she never was alone. Before Captain Frederick had gone to meet his maker on the point of a Matabele spear he had left behind four young Gilstraps: Honoria, Gladys and Helen; and Horace. Honoria, Gladys and Helen were schoolgirls at a select establishment in town, and they had the manners of schoolgirls. Whenever Elijah called on their mother they sat in the window seat as if chaperoning her, ostensibly reading books or sewing, but each time he risked glancing their way one or the other would be lowering her eyes demurely and they would all be sniggering – no, tittering. They laughed with tongues and teeth, through slotted lips.

Horace did not titter. Rarely around when Elijah arrived, he nevertheless contrived always to be there when he left, lounging in a doorway, against the wall beneath the stuffed and mounted head of a doleful wildebeest, propping up the newel post in the hall, wordlessly smirking. Elijah always had ready a few smart ripostes to any insult Horace should care to utter, but Horace never did utter so Elijah had to remain silent in the face of the unassailable smirk.

The maid let him in, indicating that he should leave his umbrella in the porch, it being unworthy to associate with the Gilstrap gamps in the elephant's-foot stand in the hall. 'I'm Strict and Particular Baptist,' she had informed him the first time he called and announced his errand, as though he had proposed to convert her on the doorstep.

Mrs Gilstrap received callers in the drawing room to the left of the hall. When Elijah was shown in she rose, swaying slightly, and extended a damp hand. She always did and he never knew whether he was expected to shake it or kiss it. The former seemed about as much as duty demanded.

'Do sit down,' she said. There were enough chairs in the drawing room for her to have hosted her own committee meeting. Elijah cautiously chose the most repellent, a horsehair spoonback with legs so short and arms so low only a gorilla could have relaxed in it. It would never do to start lounging, as he might in one of the overstuffed armchairs. Relax on horsehair and you could find yourself slithering to the carpet. As he sat down one of the springs twanged melodiously and a muffled snort betrayed Helen Gilstrap uncoiling from the hearth rug and heading for the window seat. He could have sworn that the window seat had been empty when he entered, but there they were, all three of them, Honoria, Gladys and Helen, poised and ready to titter.

Mrs Gilstrap sighed heavily.

'Seven years ago,' she said, 'seven years exactly tomorrow, we heard the news about Captain Gilstrap.'

'My sincerest sympathy,' Elijah said. The Congregation of Mount Horeb did not encourage prolonged mourning among its members. Deceased Horebites were said to have gone on ahead, as though the rest would catch up shortly, as indeed they would.

'And it was this evening, seven years ago exactly, that I had my premonition.'

'Exactly.' Elijah could have sworn he heard the merest ghost of an echo from the window seat. Surely the Gilstrap girls could not suppose that the anniversary of their father's death was an occasion for levity?

'We were very close,' Mrs Gilstrap continued, 'even when parted by great distances as we often were. We wrote to each other once a week, but his letters, of course, were often delayed by hostilities and the *terrain* . . . but I always knew when one was coming. The day before, just about the time it was arriving in England, I suppose, I sensed its approach' – was that a faint disturbance in the air around the window seat? – 'and I would say to the girls – wouldn't

I, girls? – a letter from Father will be with us tomorrow. And wasn't I always right?'

'Yes, Ma,' one of the daughters said, not quite loudly enough to smother the whickering of the others. They sounded like asthmatic rabbits.

'But on this occasion we had had a letter only the day before. I had a sense of great disquiet. When the telegram came I was ready for it, as though some part of my dear Frederick was coming with it. Distance could not divide us. When we were together it often seemed that we knew each other's thoughts. He often joked about the possibility of tele – telesth—'

'Teleaesthetics, Ma,' Honoria said brusquely. How had she got the word out through those teeth?

'Now I wonder if he ever tries to communicate with me from beyond.'

Elijah groaned inwardly. He was expected to make a faithful report of all conversations. How was he to get around what she was obviously trying to tell him, that she was awaiting a call from the grave? The Congregation of Mount Horeb were seriously perturbed by suggestions that spirits might be raised from the dead and addressed. Still, she had mentioned thought reading, teleaesthetics, as she had tried to call it. That *was* a rum coincidence.

Mrs Gilstrap was still speaking. 'Vibrations. Certain people are very sensitive to vibrations. After all, sound travels across vast distances, why not thought?'

Had she any idea of what she was talking about?

'Like when you put your ear to a telegraph post,' Helen observed, to no one in particular.

'Like your still small voice,' Mrs Gilstrap said.

That would go down well among the Elders. Another snuffling silence fell.

'Well,' Elijah said, when he could endure it no longer, 'electromagnetic waves may one day carry sound, why not thoughts as well?'

If that were the case the whole area might have been advised of the properties of Elkington's cod liver oil. Back in February, sitting in the reading room, he had chanced upon an article on a similar theme. He quoted it, rashly. '"Man may be able some day to communicate by wireless telephone with the planets."'

Right now that seemed as likely as wireless telepathy. From the window seat came a hollow whisper. 'Hello, Venus. Hello, Mars.'

Four

On the way out he averted his eyes from the elephant's-foot umbrella stand, noting, before he looked away, that someone had been polishing its toenails. This struck him as peculiarly repulsive. Had God, on the fourth day of Creation, fashioned the noble pachyderm in order that its feet should be exactly the right size to accommodate umbrellas and walking sticks? Whose walking sticks were they, anyway? The late captain's, retained in sacred remembrance? *Horace's*?

He was trying to ignore the presence of Horace, who had timed his materialization at the foot of the stairs to coincide, as usual, with Elijah's departure. The Strict and Particular Baptist closed the door behind him with a thud that just missed being a contemptuous slam.

The bay windows overlooked the road. As he went down the steps of the steep garden path Elijah did not need to turn his head to see the lace curtains twitch. He knew that the Misses Gilstrap had him in their sights. If he walked on down Holloway Hill to the corner of Ryecart Road they would be able to watch him all the way, and the streetlamps on Holloway Hill were plentiful and bright. Even if they didn't watch he knew he would still feel their gaze upon his back. His neck would redden inside his stiff collar, his ears would glow as he passed beneath each light.

Instead he turned swiftly at the corner of The Crescent and was out of Gilstrap surveillance in seconds. It was a curving street that cut off the corner of Ryecart Road, and there was not really enough of it to be a crescent, but by the size of the villas going up he could see that the residents were going to expect a more impressive address than Brickworks Lane, which was what everyone had called it before the building started. The houses were touched by the affluence of Holloway Hill; he could tell by the pipework at the back that they had bathrooms. The one on the corner where The Crescent came out into Ryecart Road was owned by James Roper, the estate agent, he of the map and the large ideas. This house had stood for a decade or more, erected on the assumption that Trimley Road would act as a boundary between the houses at the Holloway Hill end of Ryecart Road, and the ones like Elijah's at the Milton Road end.

Roper was a widower; his daughter Lily kept house for him with rather more income, Elijah guessed, than Agnes had at her disposal for the five of them. Mr Roper was not a member of the Congregation of Mount Horeb so Elijah was taken aback when, encountering Lily as he passed the gate, she smiled at him and said, 'Good evening, Mr Briggs.'

People rarely addressed Elijah as Mr Briggs and even more rarely looked pleased to see him, but there was a gaslight opposite the Ropers' front gate, no doubt positioned at the behest of Mr Roper, and there was no mistaking Lily's smile. He was almost lost for words.

'Good evening, Miss Roper.'

'Were you coming to see Dad?' Lily said. 'How strange, I've just seen yours.'

'Have you? What on earth for?' Elijah blurted out.

'Not for anything. We passed in Trimley Road.'

'Oh, I see. I wasn't calling – just passing, too – on my way home.'

'I suppose you've been doing good works, Mr Briggs?'

He longed to get away, he longed to keep the conversation going, such as it was, while he basked in Lily's smile. The rain had stopped, the smile parted the clouds and the stars shone through. If only he didn't suspect that Lily's smile was as artificial as Horace Gilstrap's smirk. He was sure that she was laughing at him.

'The still small voice, isn't it?'

'What?'

'Don't you go round telling people to listen for the still small voice? I had Charlie Campion here once, but Maggie sent him packing.'

The Congregation of Mount Horeb had advice for those who found themselves dealing with doubters. He recited, automatically, 'We believe that there is nothing to be gained by haranguing the unbeliever. Souls will not be brought before the Throne by threats and exhortation, indeed, threats and exhortation may harden the heart. The still small voice will speak to all who will listen as it did to Elijah on Mount Horeb. One Kings nineteen, verse twelve.'

He blushed as he always did when he had to mention the prophet Elijah by name because people could seldom resist remarking upon his own.

'The still small voice spoke to *you*?'

There she went, on cue. Oh, Miss Roper, Lily, how could you? But he was wound up now, the words kept coming.

'"And behold, the Lord passed by, and a great and strong wind rent the mountains, and brake in pieces the rocks before the Lord; but the Lord was not in the wind: and after the wind an earthquake; but the Lord was not in the earthquake:

'"And after the earthquake a fire; but the Lord was not in the fire: and after the fire a still small voice."'

'That's awfully good,' Miss Roper said. 'Did you write it yourself?'

He was shocked. 'No, I told you, it's from the First Book of the Kings – in the Old Testament.'

'And do you know it all off by heart?'

'Yes.'

'The whole of the Old Testament? I say!'

'No, not the whole of the Old Testament,' She *was* laughing at him, but it hurt less than the suppressed tittering of the Gilstrap girls. Lily's smile was bright and open, her gas-lit teeth sparkled with warmth. 'If only man will listen, the still small voice will speak to all of us.'

'Does that include women?' Lily said. 'Do come in, anyway, even if you were just passing. We can't stand here talking at the gate, it's much too chilly.'

Dumbstruck with joy he followed her up the path and she opened the front door with its stained-glass window portraying a secular subject.

'Come into the kitchen, it's Maggie's evening off. We'll have a cup of tea.'

The Ropers' kitchen was bigger than the Briggses' living room. There was a gas range; he had never seen one before, only in advertisements. Lily put the kettle on.

'Now, what's all this about being able to hear the still small voice? How do we hear it?'

'In this troublous world,' he intoned, 'the voices of commerce and idle pleasure are raised all around us. The Congregation of Mount Horeb ask that we set aside a time to listen at a certain hour, a moment of quietude—'

'What *is* quietude? I mean, is it more quiet than quiet*ness*?'

'It's a state of quiet – like beatitude, a state of blessedness,' he hazarded.

Lily looked impressed. 'That's jolly good. And why do you call yourselves the Congregation of Mount Horeb?'

'Because that's where it happened – the still small voice spoke to – to the prophet.' He wished she would not interrupt. He could keep going with some degree of unself-consciousness only if he did not have to think about what he was saying. Most Horebite candidates for conversion kept silent until the speaker shut up and went away, thoughts fixed upon the Necessary Jar. 'A moment of quietude, at a certain hour, agreed upon beforehand.'

'Agreed upon? With God? Do you take sugar? Like asking Him to telephone at four thirty?'

Don't be light-minded, Miss Roper.

'No, but our prayer meetings are held at certain times on weekday evenings. If others sit in quiet – in contemplation, at the same time, we hope that the still small voice may reach them through our agency.'

'Oh, so if I sit here and listen at the same time that you're all praying, I may hear what you're praying about? Do you come round afterwards and check up?'

'It's not checking up, but we do ask if people heard the still small voice.'

'I see.' She handed him a dainty cup and saucer, rosebud-wreathed. It rattled as he took it in his trembling hand; the spoon chimed against the cup. 'So, if I agree to sit and listen at, say, nine thirty this evening, you'll be round tomorrow to see if I heard anything.'

This was uncannily close to his arrangement with Gunnings.

'It's not an experiment.'

'But you want proof.'

'I suppose so.'

'Isn't faith all about believing without proof?'

'Of course. But if it turned out that you had heard the still small voice we would hope that you would be moved to join our Congregation.' He silently begged her to stop challenging him. Dammit, hadn't she asked him in? He hadn't been meaning to call, although he had often longed to, lacking the courage. And yet she had known his name!

'Couldn't you set aside fifteen minutes, Miss Roper? To listen?'

'When?'

'Wednesday evening, at six thirty.'

'Is that when the Horebites meet? We dine at six on

Wednesdays. Actually, I can't really manage any evening before Friday. Would Friday do?'

'There will be a prayer meeting on Friday. They go on till ten.' He put the cup and saucer down to still the agitated rattling.

'I'm sure I could manage fifteen minutes after dinner—Oh, must you be going?'

He had not been going, the tea was still hot, but he knew better than to say no, and stay. 'Friday, then, if you can spare the time.'

She saw him out, still smiling, and watched him carefully close the garden gate before she shut the door. He was sorry about that. He would not have minded feeling *her* eyes upon his back as he crossed the Trimley Road and walked the length of Ryecart Road in the gas-lit gloom.

'Well,' Elijah said, as they met in the form room, 'did you get anything?'

'I don't know,' Gunnings said. 'Was it anything to do with cocoa?'

Cocoa was one of the substances he had ruled out as a near miss. It might be liquid but it was not in the same class as cod liver oil.

'No, it wasn't.'

'I didn't think it could be. I was probably just wishing I had some. It was rotten chilly yesterday evening.'

'I know, I was out in the rain. So that was it? You sat there for ten minutes and all you could think about was cocoa?'

'No, I was getting *something*. I just didn't think it could be you.' Gunnings looked almost embarrassed.

'Why, what was it?'

'A tune. You weren't transmitting a tune, were you?'

'A *tune*? I was out in the rain—'

'You might have been whistling to keep your spirits up.'

'Well I wasn't. I was thinking. That's what we agreed, wasn't it? Did you recognize the tune?'

'"Ta-ra-ra-boom-dee-ay",' Gunnings said.

'You thought I was transmitting "Ta-ra-ra-boom-dee-ay"?'

'Not really. It's not the kind of thing *you'd* transmit, is it? I mean, it's not even the kind of thing you'd think of.'

Officially it was not. It was, specifically, the kind of thing that the Congregation of Mount Horeb was enjoined to put out of its mind. Wherever you went you heard it hummed, whistled and sung; little girls in the street, common little girls, performed it along with whoops and high kicks, imagining themselves to be Lottie Collins, knocking them dead in the London music halls. All the same, Elijah felt obscurely offended that Gunnings should believe him to be too pure-minded even to think about her and her daring performance.

'Well, what was it, then?' Gunnings said. 'Something pi, I suppose. "Lead kindly light . . ."?'

'If you must know,' Elijah said, 'it was that sign in Elkington's window – "Pure, pale cold liver oil, imported direct from Newfoundland, as free from disagreeable taste and odour as it is possible to be obtained".'

'That's a lie, you know,' Gunnings said. 'I've had the filthy stuff. It tastes like the cat's dinner, after the cat's eaten it.'

'Yes, but did you get anything? Haddock? Nova Scotia?'

'Nothing, I told you. "Ta-ra-ra—"'

'All right, all right, you don't have to sing it.'

'Do you want to try again – me doing the transmitting? I might be a natural transmitter.'

'It's not meant to work like that though, is it? Shouldn't we just sort of know what the other fellow's thinking, sort of by accident?' Elijah said. 'I was talking to someone last night – after the experiment. She said she and her husband could tell what the other one was thinking, and she always knew when there was a letter coming from him before it arrived.'

'Surprised they even bothered to write, then,' Gunnings said. 'Why didn't they just sit down and think things to each other? It would have saved a fortune in stamps.'

'It doesn't seem to work then, does it? Not for us. I think that first time must have been a fluke.' The memory of Mrs Gilstrap's confidences reminded him that he was supposed to make a full account of the meeting to his father. Given that the Horebites believed in the power of the still small voice to communicate, there was no real reason why they should not approve of experiments in telepathy, but he knew that Mrs Gilstrap's anticipation of messages from the late captain would meet with decided perturbation.

'It wasn't Mrs Gilstrap, was it?' Gunnings said suddenly.

'Are you reading my thoughts?'

'No, why?'

'I was thinking of Mrs Gilstrap.'

'So it *was* her – waiting for word from her husband. Nonnie Gilstrap always said—'

'You know the Gilstraps?' Elijah was aghast. His head was filled with their beastly feathery tittering. Nonnie? Could that be Honoria?'

'I know Nonnie, she's a pal of my sister's. Awfully jolly girl.'

Honoria, of the titter and the teeth, awfully jolly? Honoria, a friend of Gunnings? What might she have been saying about him? What might she not say in future?

Asking people if they would listen for the still small voice was bad enough. Infinitely more embarrassing was going back again afterwards and asking if they had heard it, burdened with the suspicion that the ones who said that they had were moved less by the SSV than by the Necessary Jar. If they then failed to show up at the chapel he had to chivvy them into attendance. He sympathized with their dilemma. They knew that if they admitted to hearing the SSV he, or one of the others, such as Charlie Campion, would be rounding them up for worship like an eager sheepdog, but if they said they had heard nothing he, or one of the others, would assuredly turn up again, begging them to have another try.

And some, like Henry Walker the stonemason, would not even try. Elijah preferred Henry's genial refusals to the Aubreys' cynical compliance. He did not believe, as his father did, for one minute that any of the Williams or the wife of William had ever heard the SSV. He wished, devoutly, that they would say as much and stay away, locked in their hideous conflicts behind the double gates, instead of descending upon the chapel like carrion crows when the fancy took them.

Mrs Gilstrap always promised placidly to listen and always confessed, equally placidly, that she had heard nothing. He knew *her* game. She liked the idea of chairing committees and dispensing largesse. She had no intention of joining the Congregation, she who lived at The Vista, Holloway Hill; of worshipping with men from the gas-works and the foundry, shunters and platelayers and the dregs of the Trident. Had she ever seen an Aubrey at close quarters?

And Lily Roper, had she heard anything? Twice he had walked down Ryecart Road, across the Trimley Road intersection, to the house at the corner of The Crescent. But he had not dared to ring the doorbell. Maggie the maid, whose bristly chin and loose lips reminded him of a camel, might send him packing as she had done with Charlie Campion. Lily had asked him in last time; he clung to that happy memory, knowing it would evaporate if he called again and she sent him empty away.

Five

When he came home from school on Wednesday he found Agnes fretting over a stack of boxes in the hall. It was her day for cleaning the ground floor but the boxes had arrived at ten and they had been blocking access to the front door ever since.

'I told the boy they should go straight to the chapel. He wouldn't listen.'

'What boy?' Elijah stood on the step while his sister faced him over the rampart.

'He brought them up from the station, they're from Headquarters. He just unloaded them and walked away whistling. We've had to clamber over them all day to get in and out. It's the new hymn books. What am I supposed to do with them?'

'Sing hymns?' Elijah suggested. The boxes were not large. He lifted one; it was heavy, but not too heavy for Agnes. 'Couldn't you have shifted them yourself? You could have got one of the kids to help you.'

'What was the point of shifting them; they'd all have had to come back here again. As if I hadn't enough to do. I suppose I could have put them out in the rain . . .'

'Ezra's here, isn't he? He can give me a hand. I'll put them in the cart.'

'In the rain?' Agnes did not let go of a grievance easily.

'I'll take them round straight away. Get the key of the padlock, will you? Ezra!'

His brother's angel-face appeared round the kitchen door. There was a formula for dealing with him on occasions such as this.

'Come and help me do the Lord's work.'

And of course the little tick couldn't refuse. He would have been polishing his spotless soul all day while Abby was hard at it with Agnes and the charwoman.

It was not raining so very hard. They stacked the boxes on the handcart and Ezra retired exhausted but filled with righteous satisfaction at having got wet in the cause of furthering God's Word. Elijah unchained the handcart and set out through the drizzle to tow it the few hundred yards to Cater Street. They could see the chapel from the upstairs back windows, but the garden of number 57 was one of the few locally with no outbuildings save the wash house. Roper's map of tidy squares and rectangles did not show what was really happening in the Trident. Along the ends of the gardens in Ryecart Road and Cater Street sheds and lean-tos and back-yard factories had begun to conglomerate and fuse together like pack-ice, to the point where it was becoming difficult to tell where one property ended and another began. Once they had been able to take a short cut through the back of Harboard's joinery; now they had to go the long way round, via Milton Road.

The front doors of the chapel were locked at sunset but Elijah had Father's key to the side entry. He manoeuvred the cart into the lobby at the eastern end of the building, where a flight of steep narrow stairs led up into the roof space in case anyone needed to get up there and carry out repairs. Elijah had been up to look at it several times. It was a low triangular tunnel like an elongated tent, and it had no floor, although a few planks had been laid across the joists for access. He had thought once or twice about building and storing his apparatus up there, but it would be unsafe. It was lit only by a dusty porthole at either end, and fumbling in the darkness he might put his foot through the lath and plaster ceiling into the chapel below.

There was a service to be held this evening and he could tell by the warmth as he went in that the stove had already been lit. When Father came home and learned that the new hymn books had been delivered he would assume that since Elijah had taken them to the chapel he would also have unpacked them. If Elijah went home without doing it Father would be perturbed because Elijah would have missed an opportunity to serve the Congregation, and he would have to come back and do it anyway. He would not be sent, but he would have no option. He might as well do it now.

He went into the main chapel and turned up the gas, moving across to stand before the communion table, where he could look down the aisle between the pews, so many more pews than they had worshippers to fill them. The chapel of Mount Horeb had been founded on hope and flourished on optimism. He stood where Elder Bland stood to conduct the services and raised his arms.

'Brothers and Sisters, welcome. Little children, welcome.'

That was his destiny, as Father saw it. When the still

small voice spoke, it would direct him to study to become an Elder.

His voice echoed in the empty hall. Tonight, midweek, it would be scarcely one quarter full. Even on a Sunday the Congregation rarely numbered more than 150, and in those boxes, waiting to be unpacked, were 300 hymn books with quarto pages and thoughtfully large type for those worshippers who found reading difficult or uncongenial. There would be tracts and leaflets as well. Headquarters in Halifax never missed an opportunity to offload more paper on to its outlying missions. The old hymn books had been put out in readiness for this evening's meeting, all 150 of them for perhaps fifty worshippers. He moved along the pews from side to side, gathering them up. When the Cater Street mission had opened they had been donated by other Congregations; some of them were very old and all were nasty, as decrepit as the books in the reading room, limp covers cracking away from the spines, pages dog-eared or loose, fluttering to the ground as he lifted the books.

His books clumped on the bare pine boards. He broke open a box and retraced his steps, laying out the shiny new hymn books, seven to a pew: *Canticles of the Congregation of Mount Horeb*. He stacked the rest in the double-fronted cupboard behind the harmonium, along with the tracts and pamphlets. Now to dispose of the old ones. Personally he considered them fit for the dustman, but the Elders had a horror of throwing anything away. The books would have to be stored in case another mission, even more strapped for cash than this one, put in a plea to

Headquarters. Then someone at Headquarters would consult a ledger, notice that the chapel in Cater Street, Lembridge, had been sent new hymn books in September 1894 and the horrible things would be dispatched to grace yet another set of pews. Up in the cupboard off the stairs to the roof there were stacks of old Bibles, even older hymn books, undistributed tracts and League of Abstinence literature.

He put the hymn books in the empty boxes and carried them up, two at a time. He had to take an oil lamp on ahead as there was no gas fitting in the cupboard or on the stairs, and he stood in the doorway of the little room, looking round its nine feet by four. An amazing amount of stuff had found its way up there; the shelves were already overflowing. A table was wedged in at one end with a chair tucked under it. This was where devoted Sisters of Dorcas sat with a glue pot, repairing the Bibles and hymn books that could be saved, but it was not a job that got done very often. He was tempted to put some of this lot beyond salvation and save everybody's time instead.

He shifted books and made room for his own consignment. Then he looked at the table again, at the shelves. It was not only books that they hoarded; the Horebites never threw *anything* away: piles of flaking sheet music, empty boxes, empty oilcans, empty jampots, broken book rests, dismantled gas fittings, lampshades, coffee-essence bottles, a strange iron thing that might have been a spare part for the stove, a lantern . . .

You could leave anything here, he thought, and no one would notice. Even if they did notice they were unlikely to know what it was. He could come here wherever he liked under the guise of repairing hymn books – he might even repair a hymn book or two as a way of paying rent for his use of the place.

For after all, electromagnetic waves would pass through walls. This could be his laboratory.

Father was perturbed. He had been reading Elijah's account of his call on Mrs Gilstrap.

'Tell me again,' he said. 'Tell me exactly what happened. Remember, the Lord knows what is in your heart.'

In other words, Elijah thought, don't lie. Why not say so? He said, 'Mrs Gilstrap thinks that she and her husband could communicate by telepathy – she calls it teleaesthetics. Now he's dead – gone on ahead – she's hoping he will go on doing it. All I said was that electromagnetic waves may carry sound, perhaps one day they will carry thoughts. We were talking about the still small voice. I was only being rational.'

'Rationalism is the enemy of faith,' Father said, 'and spiritualism is an abomination. Why were you even discussing it?'

'Because I thought I'd had a telepathic message,' Elijah said. 'Nothing to do with spirits. I heard a still small voice but it was only Reg Gunnings.'

'This is blasphemy.' Father was on the edge of something more than perturbation. 'There is one voice only. Go to your room and listen for it.'

'Mayn't I go to the chapel instead?'

'God is everywhere,' Father said. 'The chapel is a place

of communion where we may gather together. You may hear the still small voice at any time, in any place, but yes, I believe that you are in need of fortification. Go and sit in the chapel if you think it will help you. Elder Campion has called upon Mrs Gilstrap and explained to her that you were in error. From what she told him he deduced that you had been attempting to furnish a *natural* explanation for the still small voice. You must know that there is none.'

Don't I just?

He strode muttering through the misty darkness. Damn Mrs Gilstrap, loose-tongued old bat. He could have sworn that she was taking no notice at all of what he was saying. Perhaps she hadn't been, perhaps it had been one of her sly-eyed sniggering daughters. Well, damn them too, damn and blast Honoria and Gladys and Helen Gilstrap, damn them to everlasting torment, and while you're about it, take Horace—

What a pity his attempts at telepathy had failed. With thoughts like these he could have had the entire Gilstrap family writhing on the red Turkey carpet in the dining room, expiring all over the tiger-skin rug with glass eyes.

He was in Milton Road now, level with the entrance to Arthur Street, on the far side, where Gunnings lived. He could see the house from here, with lights in every welcoming window. Without breaking his stride he changed direction, crossed the road and approached the house, not even giving himself time to feel guilty. Why should he feel guilty? He had said he was going to the chapel. He *was* going to the chapel; he just had something to do before he got there. Nothing had been further from his thoughts when he left the house so, he told himself, this did not count as deceiving Father. It could only be accounted a lie if he had had deception in his heart when he spoke.

'A fellow can change his mind, can't he?' he said to himself as he walked up the front path.

Gunnings leaned over the banisters when he heard Elijah's voice.

'Come on up. I say, you haven't come to convert me, have you?'

'Stow it,' Elijah said. 'When have I ever—?'

'Don't get waxy. I just wasn't expecting you – thought you must be doing the rounds of the heathen.'

'Not here,' Elijah said. 'Look, I've thought of somewhere I can use as a lab. I want to shift the stuff – and there's time to do it now.'

'Huh. My hovel's not good enough, I suppose.' Gunnings gestured around his well-appointed bedroom.

'Of course it's good enough but, well, it's yours, not mine. I can't just walk in and get at my stuff any time I feel like it, can I? How'd you feel if you had to keep your camera at my place and develop your plates in a drain?'

'Fair enough. But what's the rush?'

'I've got an hour – before the committee meeting—'

'Oh, you're on a committee now, are you? Fallen widows?'

'No, but the chapel's empty till then. This place I've found – it's in the chapel.'

Gunnings whistled long and low. 'That's pushing your luck, ain't it? You going to set up your traps on the altar?'

'We don't have an altar. No, it's a cupboard, but it's so full of junk no one will ever notice if I add to it. Can you give me a hand carrying it over – I say, you won't tell anyone, will you?'

'Tell who?' Gunnings looked honestly mystified, but it was the revelation about his sister knowing Honoria Gilstrap that had made Elijah doubly anxious to find somewhere of his own for the apparatus. He didn't suppose that Gunnings would gossip behind his back, but anyone who found Nonnie Gilstrap awfully jolly must be a sad judge of character.

They could have done with the handcart, but by making two journeys with hatboxes borrowed from Mrs Gunnings, they transported the friction machine, the battery and the home-made galvanometer, the bar magnets, ring coil and Leyden jars.

'This isn't *it*, is it?' Gunnings said, when he saw the cupboard.

'What's wrong with it?'

'As a cupboard, nothing. I thought you were going to use it as a lab. There's no room in here to swing a cat.'

'I'm not going to swing cats. The point is, it's hardly ever used – look at that rubbish on the top shelves. I bet none of the Congregation's ever seen a galvanometer or a Leyden jar – stop waving that lamp about, put it on the table. It smokes like Gehenna. Now look, you can't see anything from down here, not with all those shadows.'

'I'll tell you what,' Gunnings said, 'you're going to stifle in here. Look at the flame.'

The oil lamp was flickering. Elijah had made sure it was filled, and wick trimmed. What was wrong?

'Air's getting very thick,' Gunnings said. 'We're exhausting the oxygen supply, us and the lamp – and that door's a snug fit. You'll have to leave it ajar.'

'Can't. Someone will smell the oil – and these experiments raise a stink.' Elijah saw his wonderful plan in ruins.

'You'll need ventilation,' said Gunnings. 'What's on the other side of that wall?'

'Nothing – well, someone's back garden, I suppose.'

'Open the door a crack before we both pass out.' Gunnings went down on his knees and crawled under the table. 'This paint's exactly the colour of boiled spinach – but look, you can knock out a couple of bricks down here and no one will see. There'll be an outer skin – do the same with that. Bring a mallet and chisel and chip away the mortar, then when you've finished working in here you can put the bricks back in position and no one will know.'

After Gunnings had left Elijah went back up to the cupboard, placed the ring coil on the table and stood before it. If the Hertzian waves could carry sound then continent might speak to continent, if not to planets (Hello, Venus. Hello, Mars). He knew what Hertz's apparatus had comprised; he would make his own. As Faraday had written, it was not enough to know the principles, one must experiment. Lodge had done something similar to Hertz using Leyden jars. Elijah already had enough apparatus himself to do that.

Lifting the ring coil, he saw himself in a real laboratory, surrounded by a hundred pieces of such equipment laid out on benches. Fellow scientists, eager assistants, were at his elbow. Tomorrow he would stand before his peers at the Royal Institution and deliver a lecture on the transmission of sound by electromagnetic waves. He would demonstrate to his rapturous audience, and all the world would hear him.

At the beginning of meetings it was his duty to stand with a welcoming look by the open door, open in all weathers. The Horebites reckoned that on winter evenings passers-by would see the hospitable glow of the chapel interior and be drawn to enter, and once they were in perhaps they would hear the still small voice. In fine weather Elijah's smile was supposed to have the same effect. After a while he felt like one of the gargoyles on St Asaph's.

It was as chill and wet as any Horebite could have wished for this Sunday evening. Elijah stood in the porch and handed out leaflets to the incoming brethren and sisters, this evening a little treatise on the dangers of over-indulgence by Elder Brayfield, printed by Elder Foregate. Inside the hall Agnes was already at the harmonium up on the left of the communion table, pedalling out something spiritual and sedative in a minor key. Ezra stood beside her, turning the pages. Abigail would have done it better but Ezra looked the part. Elijah would have thought that something apparently comprising three notes could have been played without sheet music.

The pews were filling, the twelve Elders already seated in a semicircle behind the table. They considered it ill-mannered not to be in their places before the rest of the

Congregation arrived. Elijah thought of Prayers at school, when the masters filed onto the platform only when the whole school was in place and the Beak swept in last of all, gown rippling behind him, the way the vicar did behind the choir at St Asaph's. Even the pastor at the Baptist chapel made his entrance last. Elijah had discreetly visited every place of Christian worship in the Trident and the town, even venturing as far as Trimley, to see how others measured up to the Congregation of Mount Horeb. His courage failed him outside the tiny synagogue in Bartlett's Lane. He did not think they would let him in.

And others might be more entertaining, more dramatic – the Roman Catholics were *terrific* although he had not understood a word of the Latin that was so different from the kind he heard at school but he thought, looking over his shoulder at the row of benevolent men with their whiskers and waistcoats and watch chains, beaming at each incoming worshipper, no other denomination was half so kindly. No Horebite preacher ever threatened his flock with everlasting damnation. After 1 Kings 19, verse 12, their favourite biblical quotation was: 'This is my commandment, that ye love one another, as I have loved you.' The Gospel According to St John, chapter 15, verse 12.

They were all so kind and well-intentioned.

If only they weren't so damned dull with it— No, that was unfair. They were not dull; what drove him to despair was their refusal to engage with any idea that had not been communicated by the SSV.

In the autumn drizzle the gas lamps of Cater Street had

haloes. It was almost time to close the inner door – the outer one always stood open during services just in case a Godless passer-by might be seduced by the sweet singing and the crooning of the harmonium – but he went out on to the step to see if any latecomers might be hurrying beneath the lamps. There was one, a woman – no, a girl – no, a young lady: Miss Roper from 216 Ryecart Road. Surely not . . .

Lily Roper had been walking swiftly. She made a sharp turn to the left and almost ran across the forecourt and up the steps, where she turned and lowered her umbrella.

'May I take that for you, Miss Roper?' Elijah said, holding out one hand for the umbrella, offering Brayfield's tract with the other.

'Oh! You gave me a start, lurking in the shadows like that.' She touched a gloved hand to her agitated heart and gave him the winning smile.

Did he really look as though he were lurking? Elijah would have been downcast, but for the smile. She was joking perhaps.

'Your umbrella?'

She looked doubtfully at the other umbrellas dripping in the stand just inside the hall, all more or less identical and interchangeable.

'Someone might take it by mistake.'

'Oh, no, yours has such a beautiful handle.' It was green; it looked like jade, although he doubted that it could be. He had seen jade in the town museum, in the minerals cabinet.

'I'll see that you get it back.'

'I'm sure you will.' She handed the umbrella to him and took the tract on the dangers of over-indulgence that he was still holding out. He wished he had put it down. What could she possibly over-indulge in with that tiny waist, clear skin, those bright eyes?

'You know why I'm here, don't you?'

'To hear the Word of the Lord?' Elijah said. He did not suppose that Lily was angling for a handout from the Necessary Jar.

'After you spoke to me of the still small voice that other evening – I listened.'

'Did you hear anything?'

'I believe I did.' She left him standing there and went to find a seat. Charlie, elder son of Elder Campion, fielded her and led the way to a vacant pew; Charlie who had once been sent packing. Elijah had not been sent packing. The harmonium had fallen silent. He took one last look up and down the street, then went in, closed the inner door and tiptoed to his place in the rear pew on the left, next to Charlie.

He sat and knelt and stood to sing and sat again, and hardly knew what he was doing. He had only to turn his eyes a little to the right and he could see her, four rows ahead on the other side of the aisle: her hair, her hat, the curve of her cheekbone, her fur tippet, the ogival sweep from shoulder to hip (corset, he thought, and a light sweat broke out on his brow). She was there because of something he had said. Could he have made a convert by himself, someone who had been drawn to the service by his inspirational words? But that smile . . . was it remotely possible that she had come along because she had known that he would be there? After all his thankless efforts with the Gilstraps, Henry Walker, the Aubreys, he had brought Lily among the believers after just one chance encounter?

Of course not, he rebuked himself. It was the still small voice that had brought her here. If the Congregation of Mount Horeb were not such gentle souls he would have awaited the hand of a jealous God (Exodus 20, verse 5) to strike him down for his presumption. But the God of the Horebites, he often suspected, must be a bit of a Horebite himself, charitable, mild, slow to anger. He would never wax wroth; at most he would, like Joseph Briggs and his fellow Elders, confess himself to be perturbed. Elijah no more wanted to disappoint him than he wanted to disappoint his father.

But whatever had brought Lily Roper here, it was something that he had said. As the sermon entered its third quarter hour he risked another glance across the aisle and saw Lily's gloved hand shielding a tiny yawn. Well, she wasn't the only one: hands were rising and falling throughout the hall. Only the Aubreys, when present, would yawn openly, cavernously, audibly even, in the front pew. He had told her of the still small voice and she had listened for it and she had heard it.

He wished he could hear it too.

Six

The inner bricks came away cleanly enough. He removed four – he needed the room to operate on the second skin, where he intended to take out only one – but the outside bricks were of far better quality, better laid. When his chosen one came loose the wretched thing did not swivel as intended but fell out. He crouched under the table, staring at the hole, imagining the brick descending slowly, floating almost, into someone's back garden. Please God, not on to someone's head.

Then he realized that the dull thud that had followed the brick's disappearance was the sound of it hitting something just beneath it: a floor; it had been an indoor noise. The truth came to him simultaneously. He had gone through into another building, one of the back-yard businesses that were springing up all over the Trident. Even now, there might be a wheelwright or a stonemason standing a few feet away watching the demolition of this wall.

Stonemason; it was Henry Walker's house and garden that backed on to the chapel. He must have built one of his sheds up against the wall. Elijah put his face to the hole. Whatever lay on the far side of the wall was in semi-darkness. He could just make out the legs of a bench or a stool perhaps. Elijah felt less like a criminal. He might have broken through into Walker's shop but he had not damaged Walker's property – not that that would give the mason any grounds for complaint. Property, Henry asserted, was theft.

He ought to be able to reach the brick – he put his arm through the gap and groped, but evidently the floor on the other side was lower than the one he was kneeling on. In order to reach through he would have to remove more bricks. He had a nightmare vision of the hole getting larger and larger and then the entire wall collapsing, but after taking out three more, on his own side this time, he had enough room to reach through and pick up the stray one, panicking until his fingertips brushed it. The floor was about eighteen inches lower on that side.

While he was at it he struck a match and passed it through the hole so that he could see what he had broken into. As far as he could make out the bench was in front of the hole and above it, and under the bench were boxes and tools stacked very close to the opening, everything covered in stone dust. It might be years before Henry looked under the bench and saw that the wall was damaged, and in any case, it was not his wall.

Perhaps we ought to be charging him rent Elijah thought vaguely. He put the bricks back with one left slightly askew; that would be his air vent. The air coming in was not as fresh as it would have been from out of doors but it was full of oxygen, which would keep the lamp alight and him alive. Michael Faraday's early struggles were as nothing compared to his: he felt more like Galileo under threat from the Inquisition for suggesting that the earth went round the sun instead of the other way about.

But there on the top shelf, pushed well behind the jampots, were the Leyden jars, the battery, the jury-rigged galvanometer and, disguised by a splintered book rest, its fretwork a casualty of Charlie Campion's careless boots, the friction machine. This was no longer a book cupboard; for a fortnight now it had been his laboratory.

Why hadn't he thought of it before? He bitterly regretted all those years he had wasted in furtive visits there to read the hair-raising accounts of moral turpitude in the minutes books: the Unfortunates, the Dipsomaniacs, the Fallen Women. They had introduced him to sins he had never dreamed of committing, had never imagined were possible to commit. He had had to look some of them up in the dicker in the library, after which he began to wonder if dipsomania might not be at the heart of the Aubreys' domestic strife.

Left to himself he would have called on the Aubreys on a Saturday when he could be certain that at least one of the Williams was out, either at the match, if Lembridge Town were playing at home, or on the cart, touting for scrap, but Elder Foregate kept a record of home visits and maintained a strict rota system; this week the Aubreys were down for Thursday evening.

There was no way out of it. Elijah thought he should be able to please youth and innocence. Was he not too inexperienced to confront Williams Senior and Junior, with William the First bringing up heavy artillery in the rear and Mrs Aubrey in ambush, waiting to attack his flank. He had considered claiming that the still small voice had not told him to put his life at risk in the cause of keeping the Aubreys in the fold, and therefore it would be foolhardy to attempt it. God might have other plans for him. God might be seriously displeased if Elijah were felled by an intemperate Aubrey before the plans manifested themselves. Not for nothing were visits known as missions. The word called up images of dauntless evangelists cleaving their way through jungle and floundering across deserts, willing to suffer, die, be eaten in their quest to bring enlightenment to the benighted heathen. At least it was unlikely that the Aubreys would eat him.

On his first solo mission he had knocked at the front door, waiting for several minutes on the unscrubbed doorstep until an upper window was flung up and a head of indeterminate sex yelled at him to go round the side unless he was selling something, in which case he could sling his hook. Other suggestions followed which were suitable only for the Old Testament.

Going round the side entailed entering the yard through a wicket set in the right-hand gate. As he opened it the smell of rabbit-skin glue, which in the street had been no more than part of the general miasma, surged out and struck him in the face. Smoke rolled across the yard in acrid coils from a brazier in one corner and a smouldering bonfire in another. By the fire stood William Junior, toying with a sledgehammer and spitting into the flames. The Aubreys' horse, whose name was unknown since no one dared to ask, extended its neck over the stable door and coughed resonantly. Elijah half expected that it too would spit. Most tradesmen's horses would accept apples and lumps of sugar from the neighbourhood children. The Aubreys' horse was rumoured to chew tobacco.

By the brazier the Aubreys' dog, also nameless and for the same reason, lay stretched out, vibrating with a deep continuous growl like a purring cat. Elijah eyed it nervously and made a wide detour around it, but it only exposed a tooth and leered at him, trained to go for those who came over the gate, not through it.

William Junior regarded him through the smoke with what Elijah identified, even in the poor visibility, as an unconcealed scorn that made Horace Gilstrap's smirk seem almost benign in retrospect. Elijah thought wistfully of the drawing room at Holloway Hill. At this moment he would have preferred even the muted sniggering of the Gilstrap sisters to the sustained growl of the Aubreys' dog.

'Good evening,' he said, in the direction of the bonfire.

William Junior gave the sledgehammer a twirl. 'The 'old devil's indoors,' he said, jerking his head towards the slabby side of the house, where outbuildings clung like bracket fungi round the bole of a tree. The horse stamped its hooves suggestively and the growl changed pitch as if a kettle were coming to the boil. Elijah decided against pausing to enquire after William's spiritual health and veered towards the side door, but before he reached it, it was yanked open from inside and William Senior reeled out, followed by a saucepan lid and a salvo of advice about where he could take himself and his nasty habits. This was reinforced by a flying bottle, which caught him in the small of the back. The saucepan lid, having missed its target, continued to roll around the yard on its flange and disappeared with William Senior into the smoke, which, in a sudden squall of wind, thickened and swirled. The door slammed and Elijah heard the bolts strike home like pistol shots while William Junior's laugh ricocheted off the walls.

Elijah retreated to the gate, backing off slowly in case an unexpected movement should provoke the dog, or even the horse, which might be a man-eater like the King of Oude's fabled stallion Kunewallah, which had slain tigers. A series of descending thuds, indicative of someone falling downstairs, came from inside the house. He fumbled behind him for the latch, opened the wicket and ducked through into the street. There was nothing for it: when he made his report he would have to admit that when he called at the yard the Aubreys had found it inconvenient to stop and speak to him. He had tried to do his duty. If Father or Elder Foregate were disappointed by his lack of resolve he could mention the sledgehammer, the airborne bottle and the dog.

But they did not require of him anything they shrank from themselves. When Elijah, aged eleven, had first accompanied his father on missions, Elder Briggs had passed through the wicket and stood alone and glorious in faith (while Elijah hung back on the safe side of the gate) like Daniel in the den of lions, secure in the knowledge that the angel of the Lord would be along presently.

Perhaps, Elijah thought, making sure that the wicket was fast – for he though he heard heavy breathing on the other side and the scrabble of horny paws – when the SSV has spoken to me I shall be sure that I am in the Lord's hand, and he set off for his next port of call feeling diminished, as he so often did these days. It was not that he did not want to believe; he did want to, but wanting was not the same as believing. How dared he go among people claiming to be a missionary for the Congregation, when he had so little faith himself? Father had confronted Williams Senior and Junior in exactly the same way, in exactly the same tones, as he addressed Miss Gallow the milliner and Jack Morrell the blacksmith, who never wielded *his* sledgehammer in anger, even though he was going deaf and had to be shouted at.

And, somehow, it seemed to work. After all, did not the Aubreys attend chapel on occasions? After all, Elijah reflected, nobody else was at risk really. They seemed to assault only each other. It was the very thought of the consequences of being struck by one that made him flinch.

The next person on his list was starred in red ink, a sign that this was someone who not only had failed to hear the still small voice, but had so far declined to listen for it. Henry Walker, the stonemason, was at 33 Ryecart Road, almost a neighbour. It was his house that backed on to the chapel and his workshop, built up against the rear wall of it, into which Elijah had knocked his air vent. The downstairs front of the house had been converted into a shop where samples of Henry's work stood around, turning it into an indoor graveyard. In the window, on a bed of balding green chenille, and flanked by garlands of wax roses faded to grey, was a simple headstone, shaped as a Gothic arch, with scrolls and lilies engraved upon its polished surface. Once inside, however, the client was surrounded by looming angels, urns, broken columns and Henry's masterwork, which might not have been intended for a sacred situation, a muscular nymph, inadequately clad in small leaves. Nymph and angels alike, their faces were composed in what Henry described as Mona Lisa smiles.

'They don't go up at the corners, Mona Lisa smiles,' he explained, as though they were an architectural feature, 'so they look solemn, but seen in a different light they are cheered by the promise of heavenly glory. It's all done with dimples.'

Henry had no confidence in the promise of heavenly glory and was quite frank about saying so. Elijah thought his tolerance of Horebite attempts to convert him quite saintly, almost Christlike.

Mrs Walker, a regular Congregant in spite of Henry's unaligned status, came through from the kitchen, drying her hands on a dish cloth.

'Oh, it's you,' she said, peering between angels. 'Lord give you strength. Don't think I haven't tried. "Don't nag, woman," he says, "or I might say something I'll regret. Leave it to them Elders and I'll say it to their faces and never regret a word of it." I tell him, "As a member of the Congregation it's my duty to bring you before the throne." "Do the words *horse*, *dead* and *flogging* come to mind?" he says. "When you're up there with the heavenly host and I'm in the other place, you can lean over the fence and wave."'

Elijah was about to laugh; then he was glad that the gloom hid his widening smile. There was a tremor in Mrs Walker's voice; she saw nothing remotely amusing in her husband's sunny atheism.

'Go through,' she said. 'See if you can do anything with him.'

'God, you lot never know when to give up, do you?' Henry said when Elijah ran him to earth in one of the garden sheds where the mason and his apprentice did the letter-cutting on headstones. Because of the dust it was open on three sides and the wind, trapped in the narrow garden, blew freely through it, stirring up little white eddies of marble and alabaster powder. Henry was clearing up by the light of a hissing flair.

'Well, go on, say your piece,' Henry said. 'Not that I don't know it by heart: earthquake, wind, fire, still small voice, dee-da, dee-da, dee-da. It amuses you and it doesn't hurt me. Where was that still small voice when the prophet Elijah was massacring the prophets of Ba'al? One Kings eighteen, verse forty. That's what it was, you know, a massacre.'

Henry knew his Bible, alas. Since he had now quoted the essentials Elijah felt more of a fool than ever, reciting them while the mason went peaceably about his business, taking not a blind bit of notice.

'Couldn't you just put aside fifteen minutes?' he asked, implored rather. 'For Mrs Walker's sake?'

Henry continued oiling his chisels. 'We are perfectly content, Mrs Walker and me, content to differ, till you lot started in with your still small voice. For people who believe in a still small voice you do a heck of a lot of talking. If I added up all the times I've had to listen to Horebites blathering it'd come to a lot more than fifteen minutes, I can tell you. Now she thinks I'm damned—'

'We never tell people they're damned.'

'No, *you* don't, but that doesn't stop them thinking it, does it? Lyddy believes that when I'm finished I'll be carted off by devils to some burning fiery furnace while she joins the choir invisible. Medieval, that's what it is. "How can I be happy in heaven knowing what's to become of you?" she says, and she *cries*. "Well, obviously you'll be happy," I tell her, "or it wouldn't *be* heaven. Everlasting bliss – you'll forget all about me." Then she cries even harder. Tchaaaah!'

Elijah made a mental note to request that a Sister of Dorcas be sent round to have a word with Lydia Walker. The still small voice was supposed to bring peace and joy to the soul and yet it had made Mrs Walker's life a living misery, imagining the heathen Henry doomed for ever to the flames of hell.

He could *pretend* to hear it, for her sake, Elijah thought, but Henry Walker, though a heathen, was an honest heathen, more honest than Elijah Briggs with his secret laboratory and his ever-present schemes for inventing a message from the still small voice to get his own way.

Monotonous shrieks issued over the Aubreys' gates with the smoke. He stared down the street, where the lamp-lighter was walking ahead of him. One after another the gas flames blossomed in their lanterns. Oblivious, he passed his own front door and continued towards Trimley Road. Beyond it, the light at the corner of The Crescent sprang to life, the one outside the Ropers' house. He seldom gave much thought to the flames of hell since they did not figure largely in Horebite dogma, but now he imagined them to be noxious and smouldering, like the fires of the Aubreys' yard, while down there, beside The Crescent, was heaven, and he pictured Lily at the gate, like one of Henry Walker's angels with the Mona Lisa smile.

He had made his last mission of the evening but all the same he walked on down past Morrell's forge, crossing Trimley Road catercorner so that he should be on the right side when he passed the Ropers' gate. There was a light in the hall, behind the red and yellow stained-glass panes, but he dared only to glance from the tail of his eye in case *she* should be looking out from one of the darkened windows and see him looking in, and in case she was, he had to keep on walking, on to Holloway Hill, along and back up Union Street and Cater Street, past the chapel and round by Milton Road, before he could go home again.

Seven

J. M. Tanner at 101 High Street listed so many accomplishments and facilities on his sign board that there was barely room for his name.

GAS AND WATER ENGINEER, WHITESMITH, COPPERSMITH, LOCKSMITH, BELLHANGER AND BRAZIER. BELLS HUNG ON THE LATEST APPROVED PRINCIPLES.

It was the smithing part of the enterprise that had made Elijah into a regular if furtive customer; also the fact that Jeremiah Tanner was a Wesleyan and unlikely to consort with Horebite Elders, particularly Father who, had he known about Elijah's visits to the Tanner establishment, would have been understandably curious about the purchases of zinc, copper wire, tin foil, not least because he would wonder how Elijah was financing them. Even the soft iron armature for the induction ring had been acquired from the premises opposite, Robert Smythe (Salvation Army), a general smith who also dealt in bedsteads and fancy chimney pieces.

The financial aspect of the experiments was only one of Elijah's many guilty secrets. Agnes was permitted to dispense pocket money out of the housekeeping and she was not ungenerous, although Elijah seethed at the indignity of being subsidized by his sister instead of getting a proper allowance or going out and earning what he needed. Ezra and Abigail had a basic twopence a week, upped by a penny for every psalm that they learned by heart, with the promise of a whole shilling for the interminable 119th, which would retard even Ezra's rapidly accumulating hoard. Elijah received a flat shilling, having got the psalms under his belt at an early age, but a certain amount of this was expected to find its way into the collection plate and the Necessary Jar. Elijah had recently taken to giving himself change when he made a contribution to the Jar. Once or twice the contribution had been less than the change.

Previously all the components had been small enough to hide in his satchel or about his person, but the next experiment called for something more ambitious: two metal spheres twelve inches in diameter and two smaller ones. He imagined that they would resemble ballcocks. Who better to apply to than a water engineer? The lavatory at 57 Ryecart Road had been installed by J. M. Tanner, with a resonant cistern that clanged like a bell when the chain was pulled. If he could afford it, perhaps he would persuade Tanner to make the spheres in two halves, for ease of concealment, to be screwed together by a thread, so that he could get them into the laboratory unobserved.

The plan was to replicate Hertz's original apparatus of 1888 and produce an electromagnetic wave. He had already decided to do a trial run, like Lodge, with the Leyden jars, while he saved the cash for the spheres.

It was fortunate that the senior members of the Congregation were on the short side, stout and past the age of wanting to clamber about, and that he himself was quite tall. The various pieces of apparatus distributed around the topmost shelf were well back against the walls where no Horebite, standing where most people stood – on the floor – would see them. Since the only illumination in the cupboard was the oil lamp, shadows were thrown upwards, and Elijah had noticed that people rarely looked upwards anyway. But those twelve-inch spheres might present a problem if he could not take them apart for stowage. Still, it was less of a problem than trying to keep them hidden in his room with Ezra poking about devoutly.

He had tried to persuade Ezra that it was unChristian to pry into other people's business but unfortunately neither Jesus Christ nor Moses had ever said anything on the subject. There was no passage in either Testament that read: 'Thou shalt keep thy miserable nose out of thy brother's belongings, yea, and his ox also, lest he smite thee with sore boils.' He had tried another tack. 'Only cads go poking about in other fellow's things. No gentleman would.' But that cut no ice with Ezra.

'We are not gentry,' Ezra had lisped with his eyeballs turned upwards. 'We are all equal in the sight of our Father in heaven.'

Wait till he goes to school, Elijah thought savagely. He'll hear plenty about ungentlemanly behaviour and all this rot will get kicked out of him; but for the moment Ezra and Abigail did their lessons with Agnes, who sat darning socks or knitting while reading to them from Sharpe's *History and Geography*. History began with the

Creation in 4004 BC, in accordance with Archbishop Ussher, and ended in 1842 with the great fire of Liverpool. In between history and geography she quizzed them from Mangnall's *Questions*, of about the same vintage.

'What is common or train oil? The fat of whales. Where is rice principally grown? In Egypt, China and the East Indies. The natives of these countries make it their chief food. Whence have we tea? From China; it is the well-known leaf of a tree . . . What is coffee? How is the best ink made? What is rhubarb? What is ipecacuanha? What is Fuller's earth? What are sponges?'

Sponges are small children who soak up anything you tell them, was Elijah's verdict. He thought it frightening that in this year, only six from the end of this century of headlong progress, his little brother and sister should be force-fed like Strasbourg geese this endless, flavourless diet of facts that they could remember without ever understanding and regurgitate on demand, undigested, when there was so much to know, so much to discover.

Elijah and Agnes had done lessons at home with Mother, but Mother had known how to teach, and when Elijah was sent to school at eight his classmates had had to catch up with him rather than the other way about. Agnes might have done well at school, too, but by this time three more babies had been born and died; Abigail lived, then there was a still birth, then Ezra, and Mother had died. Agnes's childhood was over.

Mother and the babies lay in the new cemetery at North Lembridge, the end of the tram route. Horebites did not believe in elaborate memorials; Henry Walker's excesses were an abomination in their sight. They marked their small headstones with initials only and rarely visited graves, but occasionally Elijah took the tram to the end of the line and went to look at the little plot where Mother lay with his sister and three brothers.

Why didn't Father send Ezra and Abigail to school? Did he think that perhaps Agnes did not have enough to do? Elijah's education cost him nothing since he had won the scholarship to the Endowed School. If he could not afford to pay for the children there was always the Board School in Trimley Road. It could not be, could it, that he did not want Ezra and Abigail associating with workhouse brats and the sons of men from the gasworks, the daughters of Mrs Sales the washerwoman and Jack the blacksmith's twins? Were we not all equal in the sight of our Father in heaven?

He knew that he was unjust; rational but unjust, and rationality had no place in the Horebite creed. Father would never believe that his offspring were in any way superior to the neighbourhood kids – the fact that he had chosen to live among them was proof of that – but he would fear for their immortal souls. Among the neighbours were Anglicans and Wesleyans and Roman Catholics and every variety of Baptist, none of whom seemed to believe in the efficacy of the still small voice. Elder Briggs trembled at the thought of Elijah associating with freethinkers like Gunnings; there were atheists abroad in the universities, which was why, when Elijah was sent to listen for the still small voice, there was never any suggestion that it might tell him to stay at school for another two years and try to get accepted at the University of London.

In the evenings after supper Agnes, or Father if he was at home, read aloud from the Bible. This had been going on for as long as Elijah could remember; they must be on the third or fourth circuit by now. Nothing was ever omitted: the 613 commandments, the abstruse laws in the Book of Leviticus, the tables of genealogy. Tonight Agnes was embarking on the Song of Solomon, having assured Abigail and Ezra that it was a parable of God's love for the faithful. Her reading was as monotonous as her harmonium playing; she seemed to find no pleasure or even meaning in the words, which was perhaps just as well.

> 'While the Kind sitteth at his table, my spikenard sendeth forth the smell thereof.
>
> 'A bundle of myrrh is my well-beloved unto me; he shall lie all night betwixt my breasts.
>
> 'My beloved is unto me as a cluster of camphire in the vineyards of Engedi.
>
> 'Behold, thou art fair, my love; behold, thou art fair . . .'

For some reason he found himself thinking that it must be about a month since that evening when Lily Roper had come to the chapel.

'Is that it?' Gunnings said.

'What do you mean, is that *it*? Do you realize what *it* was?'

'Do it again.'

'I can't, not until I've recharged the jars.'

'Funny smell,' Gunnings remarked. 'Ozone.'

The oil lamp flickered. They had turned it down as far as it would go and without its warmth the cupboard was dank and chill. Elijah felt tongues of cold air lick his ankles from the hole in the wall under the table, but he had done it. He had discharged his Leyden jars, and across the gap between the terminals a spark had leaped. He had produced – no, excited, that was the term – an electromagnetic wave. He could not have been more excited himself than Lodge must have been when he first performed the experiment; and he had a witness.

Some witness. 'Is that it?'

'Do you realize where it's gone?'

'Where's what gone?'

'The wave. Look, that spark was just the beginning, it's over, but the wave's gone out—'

'Out where'

'Out – out – *there*. Through the wall, through Henry's shed, through the roof. It just keeps going, into space. If it was carrying a signal—'

'How do you know?'

'What?'

'How do you know where it's gone? How do you know it's there?'

Elijah was beginning to wish he had not invited Gunnings along to share this precious moment.

'Because I *do* know. I know we're breathing oxygen, so do you. We can't see it; we know. If that wave *was* carrying a signal, a receiver could pick it up. What I need is a second apparatus, that's what Hertz had.'

'I'm not sure that we are breathing oxygen,' Gunnings said. 'It's thick as mud in here.'

Down below a door opened and closed. A throat was cleared. Boots could be heard purposefully crossing floorboards. Elijah froze. Gunnings, who did not take the gravity of the situation seriously, struck a pose of abject terror, eyeballs turned upwards, hands clasped. The sound receded – whoever it was had gone into the committee room – no, they were coming back, the door at the bottom of the stairs was opening, footfalls ascended.

There was no time to dismantle the apparatus. In two leaps Elijah was on the chair, on the table, sweeping up wires and jars as he went and thrusting them to the rear of the top shelf. When the door opened the Elder Campion looked in, Elijah was sitting at the table with the glue pot in his hand. Gunnings had vanished. Where . . . ?

'I smelled oil,' Elder Campion said. 'I thought someone had left a lamp burning up here, very dangerous with so much paper about. What are you doing?'

'I had half an hour to spare,' Elijah said with a simper that Ezra would have been proud of, 'so I thought I might repair some of these hymn books we put up here the other week' – a hand closed round his ankle and squeezed gently; he resisted the impulse to kick – 'in case some other Congregation is in want,' he added.

He rose to his feet in deference to the presence of an Elder and felt Gunnings let go of his leg. The lamp cast a whale-shaped shadow on the wall as its light was blocked by Elder Campion. Thank God the lamp was burning low. He forced himself not to look upwards. If he did Elder Campion would look up too and Elder Campion was facing the shelf where the friction machine was stowed. He dared not look down, either.

Elijah thought that he might be commended for using his spare time to repair irreparable hymn books but Elder Campion said only, 'I see from your report that you again failed to make any impression upon Henry Walker.'

Sober, hard-working, easy-going Henry was held to be at greater risk of perdition than the choleric, shiftless Aubreys, for the Aubreys had come before the Throne. That they had to be rounded up periodically and brought in again, like straying sheep, only made them more dear in the sight of the Elders who, like the angels of God, rejoiced in a sinner that repented (St Luke 15, verse 10).

A sensation around his feet made him sure that Gunnings was untying his bootlaces.

Elder Campion departed, leaving the door open, and stumped down the stairs calling a warning over his shoulder. 'You must allow for ventilation. Sister Blewitt once shut herself in and was discovered in a *swooning* condition.' This time the door of the committee room closed and stayed closed. Elijah turned and delivered his kick.

'Hey, draw it mild,' Gunnings protested, unfolding from under the table. 'I was only passing the time.'

'Tying my laces together. God, if he'd seen you—'

'No thanks to you he didn't. You were too busy hiding your rotten apparatus to worry about me.'

'I had to hide it. You don't know what they're like. I'd never hear the end of it if they found this stuff.'

'I thought *I'd* never hear the end of it. That old ass on this side and whatsisname on the other.'

'What?'

'Through the hole. That stonemason chap, going on and on about the dawn of Socialism. I could have got his leg too – that wouldn't half have made him jump. How do I get out of here?'

'The way you came in,' Elijah said. 'Just go down quietly.'

'Suppose I run into another Horebite? This place is crawling with them.'

'I'll see you out,' Elijah said. 'If we do meet anyone I'll say you've been helping me mend hymn books.'

'Where's the old windbag now?'

'*Will* you shut up? He's in the committee room. Probably doing the accounts.'

'Cooking the books?'

Elijah got him off the premises and went back upstairs. He had planned to charge up the jars again, excite another wave, but what was the point if he could not detect it? He might as well carry on mending hymn books.

One thing was clear: he dare not bring Gunnings here again. Not only was Gunnings hopelessly unable to imagine what it would have meant for Elijah if they had been discovered with the apparatus, he hadn't been all that interested or impressed by the spark. He had wanted to see it done again, but only in the way he'd want to see a magic trick done twice. He would never be the colleague that

Elijah longed for, working alongside him as they sought new discoveries together.

Gunnings was all right, a good pal, a good companion, but outside school he cared for little but his photography and – Elijah liked hardly even to whisper it – billiards. Father would be perturbed if he thought that Elijah was consorting with a billiard player. A saloon had recently opened above the Co-operative stores in Trimley Road. The Elders inveighed against it (mildly) at every opportunity, and against the Co-op. They had heard that it was run by Communists.

Charlie Campion? No, Charlie was decent enough, willing; he'd be interested all right but – and Elijah hated to say it, even to think it of a fellow Horebite – Charlie's intellectual lamp burned dim. He would be able to carry out instructions, he would do whatever Elijah told him to do, but he would never understand what they were doing or be able to take it further. Anyway, Charlie would blab.

He ran through a mental list of other Horebite offspring. He was more or less restricted to them because aside from Gunnings, who was almost a neighbour and didn't care what anybody thought, most of his school mates affected to despise the Trident and especially Horebites. They found it unnatural that anyone of Elijah's age should be called Elijah. At school he was known as the Prophet, shortened to Prof. People who did not know the facts assumed that it was short for Professor and thought that Elijah must be a swot.

Well, wasn't he? Even though he was on the despised Modern side, doing mathematics and book-keeping, he worked as hard as anyone, in school or out. Much good it was doing him.

What about Horace Gilstrap? If he knew that Briggs was a man of science rather than religion, might he not put aside his contempt and pay attention?

It did not have to be a *male* colleague.

There was always Lily Roper. Could she be Ada Lovelace to his Faraday?

> Behold, thou art fair, my love; behold, thou art fair . . .
>
> Thy lips are like a thread of scarlet, and thy speech is comely:
>
> Thy temples are like a piece of pomegranate within thy locks . . .

In a fit of agitation he fell upon a hymn book and destroyed it utterly.

Eight

'Remember, Elijah, the Lord knows what is in your heart. Are you able to tell us anything about this?'

Well, of course he was, but how could he begin to tell it?

The apparatus was laid out in several pieces on the table in the committee room, the small one behind the screen where the spirit lamp and the tea things were kept. Elder Briggs, Elder Campion and Elder Foregate stood around it with Mrs Elligot, senior Sister of Dorcas, she who had discovered the induction ring, the wires, the Leyden jars and the galvanometer and had come flapping down to the meeting of the Widows and Orphans of the Fallen Committee to report that there was a bomb in the book cupboard.

Elder Foregate, who was young for an Elder and spry, had sprung up valiantly to investigate, filled with thoughts of Anarchists and Fenians, followed, after a prudent interval in which no explosion had occurred, by Elders Briggs and Campion. And Elder Briggs had noticed that alongside the galvanometer lay a notebook written up in a hand suspiciously like his son's. Elijah, filling a scuttle from the coal heap in the cellar, had been summoned aloft.

'This is your work, is it not?'

'Yes, Father.'

'What is it?'

'That's an induction ring.' What had Sister Elligot been

climbing on the table for? He tried to picture the scene and failed. What on earth had made her think it was a bomb? Why would anyone want to blow up the Mount Horeb Mission chapel?

'And this – and these? Elijah!'

'Leyden jars.'

'For what purpose?'

'They're for generating electromagnetic waves for the transmission of signals,' Elijah said.

'A scientific experiment?'

'Yes.'

Father could not have looked more perturbed if Elijah had confessed that yes, it was a bomb, and he intended to blow up the Town Hall, mayor and corporation with it.

'You were conducting a scientific experiment on consecrated premises in a covert manner – no, a deceitful manner. This is what you were doing when you told me that you were listening for the still small voice.'

'And repairing hymn books,' Elder Campion chipped in.

If only they were alone, if only Father had discovered the bomb for himself. For a start, he probably would not have thought it was a bomb, but more especially, Elijah would have given anything to spare him the shame of learning, in front of witnesses, that his son had disobeyed him, had lied to him. He could sense that Mrs Elligot was dying to go home and tell everyone, in suitably scandalized phrases, what Elijah Briggs had been up to in the book cupboard. Then he said something so unpremeditated that it might have been inspired by the SSV itself.

'But Father, I *was* listening for the still small voice.'

'Elijah, I have told you, often, scientific curiosity is not compatible with the contemplative mood. Men of science have enquiring minds – I am not entirely unacquainted with such things, I do not condemn them, but they are not for us. *We* are commanded to listen, not to think; to hear and not to question.'

He knew that Father was wishing as much as he was that they were alone. How could he argue with him in front of Campion, Foregate and Elligot? But the inspiration was strong in him. He had been shown a way out; he had to take it, and the Old Man could escape with him.

'Father, this is only the agency. Of ourselves we can create nothing' – years of exposure to Horebite sermons oiled his tongue – 'electricity is not made by man, light is not the work of man. The first Word of God was, "Let there be light." We don't *make* electricity, it exists. The Lord created it. We have only discovered it.'

He could hardly believe how well he was doing, but so far it was no more than the truth, the truth of science *and* religion. Electricity, light, pre-dated humans by aeons.

'It is in the lightning. This – what I make – is only a little lightning, and I don't actually *make* it. Isn't the hand of God to be found in all His creation? Why shouldn't the Word be carried on electromagnetic waves? I did not create the wave, I brought it forth, as Moses brought forth water from the rock.'

He saw a gleam of hope in Father's eyes. If he could save them both, the sinner and the sinned-against, he might save the apparatus too.

Elder Campion, who was not very much brighter than Charlie, was struggling to come up with something along the lines of, If God had meant us to hear electricity he would have given us lightning conductors instead of ears. He said, petulantly, 'Gaslight is the work of man.'

'No, sir. Man only liberates the gas from the coal – and I liberate the wave. I had to do this in secret in case it didn't work. While I generate waves I think – I listen – to receive the still small voice. Instead of a receiver to detect the wave I use myself. And the waves aren't confined to the cupboard. They can pass through walls; we cannot know how far they go. If the still small voice is in them, anyone can receive it.'

For true believers in the unprovable they were all looking remarkably sceptical. As far as they were concerned Hertzian waves were as spiritualism: witchcraft and a deceit of Satan. The Congregation of Mount Horeb was, scientifically speaking, still in the Dark Ages.

'And has anyone received it?' Elder Foregate said.

'Yes! Miss Lily Roper – you know the Ropers, at the end of Ryecart Road. I asked her to listen for the still small voice and afterwards, for the first time, she came to an evening service.'

'What makes you think that this – this *contraption* had anything to do with it? The Lord has been speaking to his people for thousands of years without using electricity.'

Coming from an Elder, even from Elder Foregate, this was perilously close to levity.

'But how do we know he wasn't using electricity? Nothing is created without a purpose. What I thought was, if we had this apparatus by us while we gathered to meditate, we could transmit the Word; if the still small voice spoke only to one of us, the rest would receive it. At the exact hour I asked Miss Roper to listen I was up here, inducing waves.'

This was an outright lie, but no one noticed. He did not blush or tremble. He was becoming hardened in moral turpitude.

'You have not been swayed by Mrs Gilstrap, I hope,' Father said. 'Mrs Gilstrap is in error. Teleoscophy is submitting to dark forces.'

'Telepathy,' Elijah said. 'What is the still small voice if not telepathy – the exchange of feeling – not *thought*,' he added. God forbid that they should believe that anything so profane as a thought had crossed their minds.

Finally Father got rid of Foregate and Elligot and they faced each other across the table, where the apparatus still stood, disassembled, beside the spirit lamp, the kettle, the teapot and crockery. Campion, refusing to be dislodged, poked and fiddled at it.

'I misjudged you,' Father said.

Elijah's feeling of elation after his high-wire walk from disgrace to approval had not lasted. He had lied to the Elders, in chapel, but worst of all he had lied to his father. The Old Man had not misjudged him, he had been entirely correct in his suspicions, and yet, how had Elijah lied? *Had* he lied? The fact that he had been making it up as he went along did not mean that none of it was true, and it was close enough to the truth of the Horebites for them to have believed it, especially after he had discharged the jars and they had seen the spark.

He had not been lying about gas: it was not man-made; they all saw the hissing jets ignite from fissures as coal burned in the grate. Three hundred years ago no one had known that gas of any kind existed, but now man produced it for himself – liberated it, rather. From coal came the gas that lit streets and homes – and chapels. The rococo ironwork crowns of the gasholders to the rear of Union Street were local landmarks. If God had created everything, he had created gas and electricity too.

'I beg your pardon.' Father was still speaking. Elijah swallowed painfully. How could he, liar, pardon the Old Man, who was as honest as the day was long, who had believed him because he could not believe that he would lie. Before he had to say anything Elder Briggs went on, 'Have you attempted to reach anyone else with this – this – with this?'

'It's early days,' Elijah said. That was true at least. 'I may even be mistaken about Miss Roper.' How was he going to get out of this?

'But she did come to chapel,' Father said, 'I saw her. If others in the Trident were asked to listen at a certain time when you were releasing the ray, we might discover if anyone else was receiving the still small voice.'

'This could be a great force for good throughout the world,' Elder Campion said, portentously. 'What a boon it is that we, our Congregation, should have been chosen to propagate it.'

In the right hands radio-telephony might possibly turn

out to be a great force for good. In the wrong hands it could be a force for great evil. In the hands of a fishmonger like Elder Campion it could be entirely useless. If telepathy did exist it might well involve radiating waves; he would not knowingly be deceiving anyone. Most people, and the Horebites more than most, had difficulty telling the difference between science and nonsense. Anything could be called science, it seemed to him, so long as no one understood it. There was even something called Christian Science. The Horebites would not be harmed by believing that their thoughts were being carried by electromagnetic waves. The apparatus was saved.

'If this works,' Elder Campion was saying, 'it would give us a distinct advantage over, over our, er . . . others.'

Elijah could se where his thoughts were going. Equipped with the most up-to-date technology, the Congregation of Mount Horeb could steal a march on its rivals in the mission field.

'It is necessary to experiment, is it not?' Father said as they walked home. 'To experiment and record the results? Isn't that what you've been doing in your book?'

'Yes, Dad.'

'Then of course I shall entrust that side of things to you. Keep careful account of our progress so that when we make known what is happening we cannot be accused of delusion.'

'No – yes, Dad.'

'It would be unwise, I think, to announce your activities to the Congregation at large.'

'Don't you think Sister Elligot may do that?'

'I doubt if Sister Elligot and Elder Foregate fully understood the nature of your apparatus.'

'And Elder Campion?' Elijah was quite certain that Elder Campion did not fully understand the nature of the apparatus.

'If I apprise him of the need for discretion he will be discreet.'

'So, I should go on using the book cupboard for the time being?' Since he had got his ventilation system up and working he had grown attached to the book cupboard. If not like a physicist in his laboratory at least he felt like an alchemist of old, beavering away in his monastic cell.

'If you are still perfecting your method it might be advisable. Meanwhile, I shall meet with the Elders and we can devise the best way to proceed. I take it that if many of us are gathered together in the presence of the apparatus, you will make the ray and we will concentrate our thoughts.'

'Thoughts?' Unspoken between them was the injunction to listen and not to think.

'Not thought, as such,' Father amended, 'but the power of our minds to express a message which the ray will convey to those who are able to receive it. You say there is no limit to the distance these rays will travel?'

'Waves, Dad. As far as is known.'

'But those closest will be the first to hear?'

Elijah wearily debated with himself how to answer. In the long run perhaps that was true, over millions of miles, but Father was not thinking in the long term. He was thinking of the Trident, and the Trident was so small an area that even someone with a megaphone on Holloway Hill would be heard more or less instantaneously in Milton Road. He was never going to be able to explain the difference to Father and the other Elders, between sound waves and electromagnetic waves. In any case, none of them would have the slightest idea of the form these waves took. Probably they imagined them like the waves of the sea. He wished he hadn't thought of that: now he could see them himself, rolling, crashing on the shore, breaking into foam. He had been to the seaside once, when he was very small, before Mother died; sent away with Agnes to avoid the scarlet fever, but when they came home the new baby was dead.

'What you must do, Elijah, is to discover among our Congregants those who are prepared to partake of our experiment.'

'Perhaps,' Elijah ventured, 'it would be better to ask people who aren't yet in the Congregation, those most in need of the still small voice.' Did he want this experiment to succeed or not? If it failed, would the apparatus still be safe? 'After all, it won't only be heard by those who are listening for it. These waves go everywhere.'

'Of course, but to begin with we need to take careful note of the results. Once we are sure that the still small voice can be conveyed along the rays, then we can extend our operations.'

Once we are *sure*? How could they possibly be sure? So far he lacked proof even of the existence of the still small voice and yet . . . hadn't Miss Lily Roper come to the chapel in response to his request that she should listen for it? He dared not let himself believe that she had come because he had suggested it.

Or had she read his thoughts? He blushed deeply in the darkness as he recalled what he had been thinking of as he listened to Agnes's flat voice reading the Song of Solomon, those rich, intoxicating words: silver and cedar, ivory, pomegranates, myrrh and milk and honeycomb, wine and leopards and lilies. Lilies.

Nine

Elijah had intended to make a label for the notebook now that he did not need to conceal it. Then he realized that it would have to contain information doctored for the benefit of the Congregation of Mount Horeb so he began another book and entitled it *The Electric Telepath*. Almost he was sorry that electric telepathy was not what he was investigating because it sounded so convincing. A convincing name, he thought, was half the battle in making people take you seriously.

Inside the book the tenor of his notes became very different because they would now be read by the Elders whom Father had taken into his confidence. If only Father weren't involved. He had no qualms at all about bamboozling Elder Campion and Sister Elligot or, indeed, anyone credulous enough to believe him, but Father, trustful Father, was a different matter.

The second Friday in November was appointed for the inaugural experiment. Four Elders were preparing themselves to participate. The apparatus was to be brought down from the cupboard, set up in the committee room and they would concentrate the power of their minds not *thinking* – while he stood before them and induced the wave. Most of the preparation, he guessed, was finding ways around the use of the word 'thought'. They had been so schooled to listen, not to think. He had assisted them modestly by stressing that the 'pathy' part of telepathy referred to feeling, not intellect.

His own preparations were far more arduous. It was his job to go around the neighbourhood persuading people that they might share in a great leap forward in the activities of the still small voice. He had to choose his subjects with care; that was how he described them in *The Electric Telepath*: subjects. They needed to fancy themselves bright enough to understand what was going on but not be, in fact, bright enough to see what was really going on, definitely not people who knew how things worked; no one from the telegraph office, for instance. They had to be genuine members of the Congregation of Mount Horeb, or patrons; not those who would agree to anything for the sake of the Necessary Jar, although from his point of view the latter would be ideal subjects. So that ruled out Joe Jarvis from Cross Street, who would have sworn he had received the entire Book of Revelations in exchange for a pint at the Bricklayer's Arms.

He was not sure about including Mrs Gilstrap. Father might not approve but Elijah could not face day after day of rebuffs without some glimmering of encouragement. He decided to start with someone he knew to be sympathetic and, possibly, receptive. On the Saturday before the scheduled experiment he changed his collar, polished his boots, put all thoughts of the Song of Solomon out of his mind and set out down Ryecart Road for the house of Roper.

When Maggie showed him in Lily Roper was seated at a dainty desk in the drawing room, frowning over columns of figures. The frown sketched a charming little comma over the end of her left eyebrow. She must know it was there for she was rubbing it out with her fingertip as she looked up to greet him.

'Oh, Mr Briggs!' He did not have time even to say good morning. 'Are you any good at arithmetic?'

He was extremely good at arithmetic. 'What is the trouble, Miss Roper?'

'These accounts of Father's. He gets me to check them for him but he's much better at it than I am. If there's a mistake I'll never spot it.'

'May I?' He approached the desk and turned the papers to face him. So that was how Roper made his pile: too mean to employ an accountant, relying on the unpaid services of Lily. He ran his eye down the columns. 'Sevenpence ha'penny missing – there, at the bottom. And I think that nine is a nought. The pen's slipped.'

'Oh, *thank* you.' The comma had quite disappeared. Her eyebrows were two circumflex accents. 'I'd never have been that. You're a godsend.'

'That may almost be the case, Miss Roper.'

'*God* sent you, Mr Briggs?'

He longed to say, 'Oh, for heaven's sake, call me Elijah,' but she might well do it for very heaven's sake.

'I came on chapel business. Do you remember that time I asked you to listen for the still small voice and you came to the service and told me you'd heard something?'

'I don't know that you could call it hearing, exactly. I was moved to come.'

'I may have been responsible for that, Miss Roper.'

'Really? Do sit down – yes, just there – were you praying for me?'

'I was conducting an experiment.'

'On me?' Two full stops of dimples appeared, one each side of her mouth; Henry's Mona Lisa effect. 'Without my consent? Mr Briggs!'

She was flirting with him. This was unfair; she ought to know better, especially at eleven o'clock in the morning.

Maggie put her camel's face around the door.

'Will *he* want tea, miss?' She jerked her head in Elijah's direction.

'Of course he will – won't he, Mr Briggs?' The camel withdrew. 'Maggie always brings tea at eleven o'clock. I can't let you go until you've told me about your experiment.'

'It wasn't just on you, Miss Roper.' She mimed roguish disappointment. 'Are you acquainted with electromagnetic waves?'

'Absolutely not, Mr Briggs.'

'Oh, do call me Elijah,' he burst out as the door handle turned and Maggie barged in backwards with a tea tray, which she put on the desk. Lily swiped the accounts books aside just in time. Maggie gave Elijah a leery look, flexed her whiskers and stormed out again. Elijah stared at the floor and wished for death.

'Of course I'll call you Elijah,' Lily said, 'if you'll call me Lily. It's ridiculous, this formality. It's not as though we hadn't been introduced. Milk? Sugar? Now, these magnetrical waves.'

'Electromagnetic.' But he did like magnetrical – it was

as good a word as any, like Dad's teleoscophy. Both might come in useful in the operation of the Electric Telepath.

'A biscuit?'

'No, thank you.' Jesus, he couldn't cope with crumbs as well. 'Electromagnetic waves. They are everywhere, like light. They may one day carry sound. I have built an apparatus by which, I hope, they can be caused to carry thought—*feeling*. I call it the Electric Telepath.'

'That sounds impressive. How clever of you.'

'It's a very simple apparatus – not difficult to make.'

'And you tried it out on *me*?'

'Not just on you. I was inducing waves and hoping that they would carry the still small voice to anyone who might be listening. What did you hear that evening? Or feel?'

'Let me think.' She touched her fingers to her chin, giving the question serious consideration. The full stops vanished, the comma returned. 'I didn't actually hear anything. I just had the distinct impression that someone was thinking about me.'

He hadn't been thinking about her, had he? He was so carried away by the image of himself at work in the cupboard that he'd forgotten the facts. At that time he had not even assembled the apparatus. But he might have been thinking about her.

'Not a sparrow falls without the Lord knows of it. We are always, all of us, in His thoughts.' There was no getting away from that word; still, surely God must be allowed to think. 'It's just that most of the time we are not paying attention.'

'And your apparatus helps Him to reach us? That's almost miraculous.'

'It's science, Miss Roper. Lily. The thing is, we hope to repeat the experiment next Friday.'

'You're going to send those waves to me again?'

'They go everywhere, they radiate. But the Elders of the chapel want to know if people really are receiving them. If you might do what you did before, listen with particular attention, on Friday evening, at seven thirty.

'I'm sure I might, Mr— Elijah. I could hardly do less, could I, after you helped me with my sums?'

'Alone today,' Mrs Gilstrap sighed. 'The young things have all gone out.'

The absence of the young things had struck him the moment he entered the hall of The Vista, Holloway Hill: no Horace propping up the newel post, which was normal, but he did not feel the unseen presence of Horace and, when he was taken into the drawing room, the window seat was empty of Honoria, Gladys and Helen. Fresh from his happy half hour with Lily Roper, free from the malevolent young Gilstraps, he was buoyant with confidence. He could convince anyone of anything. He could sell wings to an angel.

'Mrs Gilstrap, do you remember telling me that you believed you were – used to be – in teleaesthetic communication with your late husband?'

'Yes, and who did you tell?' Mrs Gilstrap said. 'I had that Elder Campion round here telling me that spiritualism was a snare and a delusion of Satan. I never said I got messages from Fred after he died – I just wish I could, I can tell you. Never got a dicky bird.'

It seemed to Elijah that Mrs Gilstrap was also a lot more relaxed in the absence of her children. Her accent had slipped too, as if she had loosened her stays and everything was joyously expanding. He was shocked by the image and felt his neck reddening.

'But you did feel you were in telepathic contact with him – before his death?'

'Telepathics, now, is it? Well, it's a sight easier to say,' Mrs Gilstrap remarked.

'Telepathy may be the next step in the evolution of language,' Elijah said. 'The Elders have no misgivings about that. In fact, that's why I'm here. We believe that what we call the still small voice may be a telepathic communication from . . . above.'

'God, you mean?' Mrs Gilstrap said, bluntly. 'You don't say!'

'It's His voice we are listening for, isn't it? I – and the Elders – have devised an apparatus which, by the use of magnetrical waves, may enable us to hear the still small voice more distinctly. We intend to attempt this on Friday evening at seven thirty. Would you be able to assist us, Mrs Gilstrap?' He was slipping into fluent Horebite now. 'Would you be able, willing, to set aside your daily cares and duties for half an hour or so, to sit and listen for the still small voice?'

'Down the chapel?'

'No, here in your own home. The apparatus will be in the chapel.'

'Wouldn't it be simpler if I just came along and listened?' Mrs Gilstrap said.

'Ah, yes, but the waves I shall induce with the apparatus may travel great distances. We have to know how far the still small voice can be carried. You are our most far-flung Congregant.'

'Far flung? You watch it, young Briggs. No one's flinging *me*.'

God, no. You would need a siege engine. Surely the widow Gilstrap was not flirting with him too?

'All right, sonny, I'll listen for half an hour on Friday. Seven thirty, was it? I suppose your waves don't carry music, do they? A bit of song and dance, now, that would be worth having.'

The front door opened and closed. Before his eyes Mrs Gilstrap drew herself up, waist in, bosom up – he could almost see the straining stay-laces. The upheaval revealed the neck of a small black bottle between Mrs Gilstrap and the cushions.

'And will that be all, Mr Briggs? So kind of you to call. Horace will see you out.'

And there, in the doorway, smirk drawn across his upper lip like a false moustache, stood the hated Gilstrap Junior.

Elijah stood up, bowed to Mrs Gilstrap who, with her back to her son, seemed almost to wink at him, and strode to the door. Was not the Lord smiling upon his venture? Only thirty minutes ago he had addressed Mrs Roper as Lily and been called Elijah in return.

'Morning, Gilstrap,' he said superbly and Horace's smirk vanished as if shaven off by one clean swipe with a razor.

* * *

'Machines will be the death of the working man,' Henry Walker said. 'First it was spinning machines, weaving machines, threshing machines, sewing machines. Soon there'll be machines to put our bleeding boots on for us. And who controls the machines? The bosses, that's who.'

'It's not a machine,' Elijah said. 'It has no moving parts, it's an apparatus. Really, man alone cannot induce electromagnetic waves.' Henry Walker would not be seduced by talk of magnetrics and teleoscophy.

'And where does the Almighty come into this?' Henry bent over his grindstone. 'Isn't he making the waves?'

'Of course He is. I simply induce them. All you have to do – if you can spare the time – is listen out for whatever message they carry.'

'Listen?' Henry straightened up. 'You listen. Lyddy goes to chapel on Sunday, morning and evening. She sits on the Fallen Widows Committee and what have you. I give my share to the funds to keep her happy. Now you want me to sit and listen to thin air for half an hour on Friday evenings—'

'Just this Friday evening.'

'This Friday evening I am addressing the Working Men's Association at the Bricklayer's Arms, upstairs back, on the subject of Capital and Labour. Pity you'll be playing with your machine, you could do with coming along to listen. I know you mean well,' he sighed, bending to the grindstone again, 'but you really are completely useless, aren't you?'

'I don't mean to be useless,' Elijah said humbly. 'Is science useless? How else would we have electric light?'

'I haven't got electric light,' Henry said. 'Don't you try to get round me by dressing up religion as science. It's the opium of the people.'

'Science is?'

'Religion is. I don't mind paying my dues to the needy because right now it's only the charitable work of your sort that stands between a lot of people and destitution. But it's not right, it's extortion. No one should have to promise to listen for voices, still, small or otherwise, to get relief. No one should have to ask for it. Food and shelter, a decent wage for a day's work ought to be the right of every working man and woman, and a pension to see out your declining years.'

Elijah wished that he dared to confide in Henry that it was in fact the other way round, that he was dressing up science as religion, but Henry was an upright man; the deception would scandalize him. Nor would he be amused to discover that Elijah's air vent came out not three feet from where they were standing, under the bench where reams of pamphlets were stacked neatly, although lightly dust-filmed, much as they were in chapel. He leaned over, selected one and waved it at Elijah.

'Go on, take that and read it. Maybe you'll learn something useful.'

Elijah was outside before he looked at Henry's leaflet: *An Introduction to the Philosophy of Karl Marx*.

Ten

Unlike the everyday missions under the direction of Elder Foregate, when he went where he was sent, Elijah had been given a free hand selecting subjects for the experiment; he could choose whom he liked. Conversely, he could omit anyone he did not like. He thought of this gladly when, cutting through Cross Street, he saw the Aubreys' horse coming round the corner at the opposite end, followed by the Aubreys' cart.

Cross Street was a short thoroughfare and he was halfway along it. He could hardly turn round and go back, pretending that he had suddenly recalled a forgotten errand in the other direction. And there were no houses on this stretch, only the back gates of the bicycle shop and Heaton's bakery on his side, and the wall of the Strict and Particular Baptist's Zoar chapel across the road; nowhere to knock and, if answered, to introduce himself and engage in earnest conversation which even an Aubrey might hesitate to interrupt.

All the time he was thinking this he and the Aubreys' horse were drawing closer to one another. Clouds of steam enveloped the horse's head; clouds of pipe smoke shrouded the driver, William Senior. As they drew level the horse clattered to a halt, harness jangling. There came a similar cacophony from the cart as the contents shuddered and settled. Elijah raised his cap to William Senior and accelerated.

'Hold hard, young 'n,' William said without removing the pipe from between his teeth. Incongruously it was a down-curving meerschaum with a pewter lid to keep out the rain. The rain was kept from William's head by a swooping sou-wester the size of a coal scuttle. It was not, however, raining. Elijah stopped and looked up attentively, one eye on the horse which, prevented by its blinkers from watching him, let him know that it knew he was there by raising its nearside rear hoof every time he moved, and rattling its headstall, which was hung not with decorative brasses but bits of shim and old cutlery.

'I've been hearing things about you,' William said. 'You and your machine.'

There is no need to feel guilty, Elijah told himself. Whatever William has heard is unlikely to be the truth.

'How you're going to send invisible rays into people's heads,' William went on. 'How you're going to shut people up in that chapel of yours and put wires in their ears till their eyeballs is fried.'

Father's assumption that the Elders and the Sisters of Dorcas would be discreet had been wide of the mark. How could he have remained so astoundingly ignorant of human nature after so many years in its company?

'It doesn't work quite like that, Mr Aubrey,' Elijah said. 'In fact, it's quite the other way about. With my apparatus we hope to reach people in their own homes by conveying thoughts on radiating waves.'

The horse tossed its head and laughed coarsely. Steam gushed.

'You mean' – William finally removed the pipe, leaned

over the edge of the cart and spat; he did it in the road so that Elijah need not take it personally – 'that instead of coming round all hours of the day and night, worrying at us to come to chapel, we can stay at home and you'll let us know what's going on?'

'Something like that,' Elijah said. 'We've always asked peoplc to set aside a time to listen for the still small voice.'

'Don't I know it?' said William.

'With the apparatus we hope that it may be easier for them to hear it.'

'So we'll be sitting round the fire, and we'll be able to hear one of them sermons without stirring our stumps?'

Sitting round the fire suggested a happy family gathered about the hearth. Elijah pictured the Aubreys crouched over one of their smouldering pyres in the yard, chucking refuse at each other in desultory fashion while vats of rabbit-skin glue simmered in the background.

'It won't be a whole sermon,' Elijah said, uneasily aware that if the Elders should convince themselves that the experiment was working, it could be only a matter of time before they demanded that he excite electromagnetic waves for an hour at a time while Elder Bland or some visiting preacher droned a sermon of even greater length because they would not be able to see their listeners yawning. 'No, to start with we shall just transmit a single verse of scripture.'

'Transmit? You using the telegraph?'

'No, this is transmission of thought.'

'What's the verse, then?'

'Eh?'

'What's the verse of scripture?'

'We don't tell people that in advance,' Elijah explained. 'That's why this is an experiment. What we are asking people to do is listen at a particular time – as we always do. Just before it is time to begin, one of the Elders will choose a verse, with divine guidance. Even I won't know what it's going to be.'

'And if it works, we won't have to come to chapel no more – we can stay at home in comfort and listen? You could be on to something there, boy.'

This was not at all what the Elders were envisioning. From their point of view the whole charm of the Electric Telepath was that the still small voice would reach a wider audience without their being aware of it. And once they were softened up, Elijah had deduced, the missionaries would move in on their newly suggestible converts.

'What we hope,' he said, 'is that people will be able to hear the still small voice even if they aren't listening for it. But to see if it works, we have to try with people who are willing to report back.'

'And was we one of them?'

'I beg your pardon?'

'Was we on your list of people to be experimented on? You and your dad have spent enough time coming round and trying to get us to listen.'

Elijah, aghast, nodded vigorously. 'Shall I put your name down, then?'

'Put us all down,' William said expansively. He jerked the reins. 'Giddap!' The horse lunged forward and the cart lurched after it, clanging hideously. 'Keep it short, though,' William yelled, over his shoulder.

'Keep what short?'

'The message. The verse. "Jesus wept!"'

'*What?*'

'"Jesus wept." Shortest verse in the Bible. They learned us that at Sunday School. I don't remember much but I remember that.'

'Friday evening, seven thirty,' Elijah called after him. William, without turning, raised his whip in acknowledgement. Elijah had never seen either Aubrey using the whip. How would they dare to? The horse would store up hatred in its heart and get them later when they were looking the other way.

He stood in the entry of the bakery to consult the list, consoled by the warm smell of bread. He already had Lily, Mrs Gilstrap, Jack Morrell, Miss Gallow, and now the Aubreys. He was about to write them down when he paused – how many Aubreys? Williams Senior and Junior, presumably, but was he meant to include William the First and Mrs Aubrey, whoever she belonged to? The thought of passing through the wicket gate to interview them after the experiment filled him with dread. Still, with Mrs Gilstrap on the very edge of the Trident and the Aubreys just across the road, he had satisfactory extremes of range.

How could he call it an experiment? Such a waste of time and effort on something that not only would not work but could not work. What would his heroes think of him and his mockery of their work – Faraday, Maxwell, Hertz himself; and the pioneers, Volta, Galvani, Oersted –

if they should be looking down at him from heaven? Mindful of Henry Walker, he had a sudden image of them lined up behind a fence, waving. Faraday especially, that good, honest, devout man. Elijah winced and shook his head to rid himself of the vision and the great men faded away, but he could still see the fence, a row of chestnut palings like the one round the allotments at the end of Cater Street.

The Elders had persuaded themselves – possibly with a view to excluding loud Sister Elligot – that those of the female sex should not be exposed to electricity. None of them could quite explain what they thought it would do to their wives, mothers, sisters; whether it was the brain that would be put at risk or some other organ. Elijah had tried to explain that no one would be handling the apparatus apart from himself.

'But the rays go everywhere, you told me,' his father said.

'Waves, Dad, not rays. They pass through walls – they pass through us. They do no harm. Only the current can cause injury and then only if the apparatus is touched. After all, women will be *receiving* the waves, won't they?'

'Yes . . .' Elder Briggs said doubtfully. 'Although I wonder if even that is quite wise. So close to the source of the influence we think is safer that no females be present.'

Elijah abandoned the argument. He was learning not to argue about anything concerning the Electric Telepath apparatus. His father's talk of 'rays' and 'influence' and 'the machine' was common to all the Elders, and his conversation with William Aubrey Senior had made him aware that a tide of misinformation was creeping across the Trident. And the Trident did not contain it.

Gunnings came grinning into the form room one morning and leered, 'Well, Prof, tell us about your machine.'

Gunnings had never called him Prof, but since the evening when Elder Campion had burst in on the experiment, Gunnings had excused himself from further visits to the book cupboard. And now that all the electric equipment had been removed from his bedroom, Elijah rarely saw him out of school.

His heart sank. 'What machine?'

'It's the talk of the billiards rooms,' Gunnings said. 'The Horebites have got an influencing machine that can tell people what to think by sending out powerful invisible rays, straight into their brains. Wouldn't be anything to do with you, would it?'

'Is that what people believe?'

'Dunno if that's what they believe. It's what they're saying.'

'The Elders found the apparatus,' Elijah said. 'You know what they think about science – it flies in the face of Holy Writ. I couldn't let on what it's really for. I can't even get them to understand about waves. I told them it might carry the still small voice to people.'

'And they believed you?'

'Oh, they believed *that*. It's what they want to believe. I had to say what they wanted to hear. Trouble is, now I've got to do it.'

'Do what?'

'Send out a wave while they all meditate on a verse of scripture and then see if anyone receives it.'

'They won't, will they?'

'Of course they won't. That's not how it works, you know that. What am I going to do?'

'Lie your way out?' Gunnings suggested. 'Same as you lied your way in?'

He did not sound sympathetic. Elijah was taken aback. Gunnings regarded his own lies lightly, but on the whole they were simple untruths, told for the sake of a quiet life. This was a huge compound fiction, growing by the minute.

'It wasn't all untrue,' Elijah said. 'I told them that God created electricity. All I do is generate it. Light is an electromagnetic wave. God created light.'

'The sun is God,' Gunnings remarked.

'What are you talking about?'

'That's what Turner said – the painter Johnny. His dying words: "The sun is God."'

'Fat lot of help that is.'

'I wasn't trying to help,' Gunnings said, and turned away.

On the evening of the experiment Elijah went along to the chapel and climbed the stairs to the book cupboard. He stood in the doorway holding up the oil lamp, feeling like Florence Nightingale at Scutari, surveying his erstwhile laboratory, regretting those happy hours with battery and coil, the Leyden jars, the friction machine; inducing currents, discharging sparks, telling himself that he was taking the first steps towards a career in science. So far he had been only duplicating the experiments of others, but once he got away, set sail on his own voyage of enquiry, what might he not discover? And what had become of his grand scheme now? One foolish lie, to save his own face and Father's, and he was embroiled in this idiotic charade.

What would happen when it failed to produce results? Would the Elders demand that he dismantle the apparatus on the grounds that he had indeed been in error to enquire instead of to listen? Or would they urge him to persist in his efforts? He foresaw a grisly cycle of visits to the Aubreys' yard and the Gilstraps. Then something even worse than that occurred to him. Whatever the results, the experimenters and their subjects might convince themselves that they had met with success. 'Isn't faith believing without proof?' Lily Roper had said to him. He knew only too well what people were prepared to believe without proof. Hadn't he himself sat for uncounted hours listening for the still small voice in the genuine conviction that eventually he would hear it?

It was a long while since he had listened; he could not remember when he had stopped, but he knew that he had absolutely no conviction that he would hear the Word of the Lord in the still small voice.

The realization gave him such a jolt that he actually shuddered and the oil lamp sent shadows swooping up the walls. He advanced into the cupboard and set the lamp down on the table next to the apparatus. There was no need to conceal it now. Even the friction machine and the galvanometer stood in open view. Did he even believe that he might receive the Word of the Lord by *any* means? He had lied and all he had felt was relief that he had got away with it; and guilt, certainly, because a lie was a lie no matter why it was told; but had he for one moment asked himself what God would think about it?

He had not lied when he said that God had created electricity and gas, and that man had only discovered them, but which God had he been talking about? Gunnings had quoted the painter Turner to rile him – 'The sun is God' – but mightn't he be right? Was not the sun the true begetter of everything upon earth, rather than the kindly, concerned God of the Horebites, who counted falling sparrows and was perturbed if he caught his followers thinking? Those old pagans who had worshipped the sun, weren't they perhaps closer to the truth? Their deity was a remote, disinterested all-father who wanted only acknowledgement – call it worship if you must – of the wonders of his creation. A deity, in fact, who looked with approval on the Galileos and Oersteds and Davys and Faradays who understood the wonders and brought them out into plain sight for all to behold and marvel at.

That god would not look with approval upon Elijah Briggs, who was afraid to count himself among the believers or the infidels, who had lied out of timidity. Was it really his father whom he had feared to hurt?

The apparatus was now set out on a tray. He hung the lamp from one finger, lifted the tray and set off downstairs. How long had he been standing in the doorway of the cupboard? He had come early to the chapel in order to have everything ready before the Elders turned up, eager to begin the experiment at 7.25, so that the apparatus should be properly warmed up, like a teapot, by the time the subjects were starting to receive. He had explained that the Leyden jars were charged already and did not need warming up; that this was the purpose of Leyden jars. The Elders did not understand about charges. They understood nothing. He stopped explaining.

He carried the tray down to the committee room and put it on the table – not the small kitchen table where Elder Foregate had set it among the tea things on the evening Sister Elligot found the bomb, but the table around which the committee members met. Ideally he should have a receiver set up to detect the wave; instead his 'receivers' were scattered all over the Trident, and whatever they thought they were receiving, they would never detect a wave.

The Elders arrived one by one, as if at prearranged intervals to escape detection, with solemn tread, hung up their coats and entered the committee room, where they took their seats in a semicircle around the table. Originally there were to have been four, but now all twelve were there. No one wanted to miss this. Elijah had to face them, standing behind the long side, to discharge the jars. As Elder Campion came in, the last, he closed the door behind him and the proceedings began. Beside the apparatus lay a Bible. There was a short, painfully courteous debate in which each of the Elders declared himself unworthy to be the One, before Elder Bland, senior by some two decades, was persuaded to officiate.

All heads bowed. Elder Bland, perhaps waiting for a hint from the still small voice, held the Bible in his two hands above the tabletop, then put it down and, with eyes closed, opened it. He placed his forefinger, after more silent deliberations, upon the page. At his first attempt the finger went into the gutter. He tried again, landed safely, opened his eyes and read:

> 'Speak, and say, Thus saith the Lord God; Behold, I am against thee, Pharaoh King of Egypt, the great dragon that lieth in the midst of his rivers, which hath said, My river is mine own, and I have made it for myself. Ezekiel twenty-nine, verse three.'

Is he mad? Elijah wondered. Am I mad? Are we all mad? I am going to— no, they think I am going to transmit *that* and people will actually receive it. They really do believe it.

'How shall we proceed?' Elder Bland enquired. There was a long silence. Elijah at last looked up, saw the solemn expectant faces and realized that the question had been addressed to him.

'As usual?' he suggested. They knew better than he did what was usual.

Father came to his rescue. 'We will meditate upon the scripture and Elijah will discharge the jars and excite the wave, and the wave will carry our thou— our meditations out into the ether.'

Elijah's spirits sank further, hearing the pride in the Old

Man's voice: pride in his son, and pride in his newly acquired grasp of technical jargon. At least he had stopped talking about rays.

'Speak the passage again,' Elder Foregate said, sensibly. Elijah guessed that Foregate wanted to hear it twice to try and make some sense out of it before he commenced meditation. 'That we may have it in our hearts.'

No, it was not sensible. It would be sensible if they opened their own Bibles at Ezekiel 29, verse 3, but no, they were fixed on the idea that the passage must be in their minds; never, never in their thoughts.

Elder Bland read the passage again, and a third time. The rest of the gathering clasped their hands and closed their eyes, but Elijah, covertly observing, saw that one after another an eyelid would rise a fraction. They could not help themselves, they wanted to watch. Overcome with affection for them and disgust at his duplicity, he discharged the jars, and when they saw the spark leap across the gap between the terminals they released such a collective sigh of emotion, or awe, or simply of pleasure, that the zephyr could have carried the message itself.

Eleven

He got the idea of the map from Roper's window and now it hung in the committee room. It was drawn to much the same scale but was only about two-thirds the size since it had a different purpose. Roper's map began at the railway bridge on the road out of town, and extended to the parish boundary of Trimley.

The Electric Telepath map had a smaller sphere of operations. Dead centre was the chapel of the Congregation of Mount Horeb, around which he had described a perfect circle in red ink. Radiating from it like spokes from a hub, or beams from the sun, ran red lines, linking the chapel to the various households in which someone had agreed to take part in the experiment. The longest line was the one that ran to Holloway Hill, seat of Mrs Gilstrap at The Vista: 1,327 yards. The shortest led to 42 Ryecart Road – 51 yards – where he had listed Mr and Mrs William Aubrey, which seemed to cover all possible permutations. The other seven households were in between, mostly at about 800 yards.

Now that the first part of the experiment was completed the map must be attended to again. There was no end to his embarrassments. After Ezekiel 29, verse 3, had been transmitted, the Elders' part in it was over. The next instalment was his alone. He now had to call on every house and collect the results. This was his punishment and he had inflicted it upon himself; or else it was in the nature of a box on the ears from his displeased God. If the Lord had had any part in the proceedings it was his divine guidance that had led Elder Bland to put his finger on Ezekiel 29, verse 3. Why couldn't it have been one of the ten commandments or, as William Senior had suggested, St John 11, verse 35.

But then, it would make no difference what the message had been, no one would have received it. He remembered what had started all this: Gunnings and the *Atlas of English History*. Suppose there had been something in that; just suppose the fact of twelve devout men, all thinking, *meditating* in concert, had caused the thought to travel around the Trident, conveyed not by the electromagnetic wave but by the mysterious agency that had caused him to know what Gunnings was thinking – but there had been no mysterious agency, only coincidence. It had begun almost as a joke. It was no joke now.

Although he said it himself – he did not say it aloud – the map was a work of art. Not least artistic was his interpretation of what the subjects reported feeling at the time of the transmission. He had been careful to edit out any mention of thoughts. Mrs Gilstrap spoke of peace and bliss and had made an unfortunate comparison with the effects of laudanum. William Aubrey Senior had reported an agitation of the spirit, or words to that effect; William Junior a headache. Mrs Aubrey and William the First were unavailable for comment.

'The headache wouldn't be the result of Hertzian

waves,' Elijah protested, for William Junior, he knew, was quick to apportion blame and even quicker to avenge himself.

'Well it weren't there when we started, it come on after about ten minutes, and went away again when the time was up,' young William growled.

'What sort of a headache?'

'Like when you been grinding yer teeth,' William said succinctly. 'Like when you been sitting in chapel with yer arse going numb, bored senseless listening to some old windbag for hours an' hours.'

Elijah omitted William Junior's headache from the record. 'Anguish,' he translated.

Miss Katherine Gallow, milliner, second only in distance to Mrs Gilstrap, had experienced 'a blessed calm and a funny smell'. Flowers, she thought, or it might have been hat paint. *Odour of roses*, Elijah wrote on the map.

To be frank, he did not much care for the results he was getting. The people farthest away from the chapel reported the vaguest responses the ones closest, the most violent, which was nonsensical. On the other hand, knowing the Aubreys, he would have expected a violent reaction in the household, since they seemed to react violently to everything, particularly each other, and hostilities were intensifying. Every time he passed the premises a row of some kind was in progress, the house and yard behind the brown-painted gates reverberating with shouts, curses, crashes and shattering glass. Had the Elders gathered around the apparatus been meditating upon the lines from Isaiah 2, verse 4: '. . . they shall beat their swords into ploughshares, and their spears into pruning-hooks: nation shall not lift up sword against nation, neither shall they learn war any more,' the Aubreys might well have been stirred to thoughts of mayhem.

He left his visit to the Ropers till last. Since Mr Roper's office was in Trimley Road and not at the end of his garden it was easy enough to check on his whereabouts. Having ascertained, on his way home from school, that Mr Roper was in his office, his unmistakable shadow striding back and forth across the blinds, hands clasped behind his back, Elijah hurried past the lighted shop fronts, dodging into the roadway to overtake slower pedestrians, skipping back on to the pavement to avoid a cart or a bicycle, past the Wesleyan chapel, the Roman Catholic chapel, the swiftly rising walls of the new Anglican church at the corner of Clarence Street, past the Cater Street allotments and on to the corner of Ryecart Road.

As he stood in the porch he prayed – although he rebuked himself at the same time for praying about anything so trivially worldly – that gaunt Maggie would be out on some errand and that Lily would answer the door herself. Through the red-and-yellow panes of the front door he saw her approaching and stood back, removing his cap as the door opened.

'Good evening, Miss Roper, Lily. Is this a convenient moment to call?'

'Entirely convenient, Mr Briggs, Elijah. Do come in.'

He followed her down the hall, not to the drawing room with the desk where she had received him before, but to a smaller parlour on the left of the kitchen door. It was softly lit. Two small easy chairs upholstered in floral cretonne matched the drawn curtains, and on a little table draped in a Nottingham lace cloth stood a bowl of flowers. He did not recognize them; they must be from a hothouse.

'It's meant to be my sewing room,' Lily said, 'but I just like to sit in here, really, when Father's not at home.'

He noticed that there were lilies on the tiles of the fire surround, white lilies on green tiles. Coals glowed in the grate.

'Why did you want to see me?' Lily said. 'Or were you hoping for Father?'

Who could hope for Father when Lily was there? Why did he have to have a reason for wanting to see her, anyway. He just wanted to see her.

'Last Friday,' he said, 'the experiment. I wonder if you received anything?'

'I'm almost sure I did,' Lily said. 'I sat in here, absolutely still, from seven thirty till, oh, at least eight fifteen. I didn't want to miss anything. I told Maggie I wasn't to be disturbed.'

'Could you tell me what you received,' Elijah said, 'even if it wasn't actual words?'

'It may have been words – not really heard, of course; *felt*.'

Not thought, naturally. But he would die of shame and joy if she had received *his* thoughts. *As the lily among thorns, so is my love . . . Thy breasts are as two young roes that are twins, which feed among the lilies . . . Thy belly is an heap of wheat set about with lilies.*

'What words?'

'Something about the Holy Spirit – heaven—'

It was a reasonable shot but the passage chosen for transmission had no reference to either. *Speak, and say, Thus saith the Lord God; Behold, I am against thee, Pharaoh King of Egypt, the great dragon that lieth in the midst of his rivers, which hath said, My river is mine own, and I have made it for myself.*

Lily must have seen his look of dismay, for the comma appeared over her left eye.

'Well, God was mentioned . . .'

It struck him, at that moment, that since he did not believe in telepathy of the natural or electric variety, he was asking her to tell him something he was morally certain had not taken place. And since it had not taken place was she perhaps trying to elicit some clue from him?

'What did other people receive?' Lily said, a shade desperately, after a long pause.

They would not be checking up on each other, that was for sure. Lily would not be comparing notes with Mrs Gilstrap or the Aubreys or Miss Gallow. No need to relay headaches, agitation of the spirit, floral odours or laudanum.

'Pharaoh of Egypt . . . a dragon . . . rivers . . .'

'Oh!' Lily leaped at it. 'I'm sure I got the impression of *water* – prophecy?'

'A prophet, yes.'

'Beginning with an E?' That was another reasonable shot.

'Not Elijah.'

'Not you, then.'

Oh, Lily.

'Elisha – *Ezekiel*.'

The only other candidate was Ezra. She'd have got there eventually. Well done, Lily. Well guessed.

'Oh, yes! The third verse, chapter twenty-nine.'

'I'm so glad,' Lily said. 'Wouldn't it be awful if I hadn't received anything?'

He bent his head, taking notes, wishing he had the nerve to look her in the eye and say, 'Lily, we both know this is absolute rot,' but he did not yet know her well enough. She might be deeply devout and truly anxious to receive the still small voice. Better still, she might simply want to make him happy. He wanted to make *her* happy.

'If you hadn't received anything,' he assured her, 'the fault wouldn't be yours. The apparatus is still in a very primitive state. We have no means of knowing yet if it will work well enough to be of use in our missions. Would you be willing to take part in another experiment?'

'Of course I would. It's very exciting, being in at the start of something scientific.'

He risked all. 'Hertzian waves may one day carry human speech,' he said. How good it felt to be telling the truth for once.

'The works of the Lord are marvellous.'

So are the works of man, he thought. 'Have you heard of Michael Faraday, James Clerk Maxwell . . . Oliver Lodge?'

'Are they Elders of the Congregation?' Lily said.

* * *

The Elders of the Congregation examined Elijah's report with deep interest. After his encounter with Lily Roper he had realized that this initial refusal to drop hints to his subjects was hindering the success of the operation. Unless natural telepathy were at work, no one would have received, felt, or even thought, anything. In all subsequent interviews he had let slip comments about Pharaoh, dragons, Egypt, rivers. All he had to do was wait until someone mentioned God – they all did, since that was a safe bet.

No one confessed to feeling nothing at all, discounting William Junior's headache, and he had to allow for the fact that sitting still and listening for half an hour was bound to admit ideas of some kind into the human brain.

Everyone was very impressed by the map, the beautifully inked streets and premises, Elijah's handwriting and the red lines radiating from the halo he had drawn around the chapel.

'Nine subjects,' Elder Foregate mused. 'For the next experiment I venture to suggest that we solicit the co-operation of others.'

'In addition to these nine,' Elijah said quickly. 'They would be deeply hurt not to be included.' This was not true of the Aubreys, who seemed impervious to hurt, even from blunt instruments, but the others professed their excitement at being involved with science, and he was getting them trained, after all. He guessed that were he to approach some of the harassed housewives of the Trident, battling against dirt and poverty and illness, he would be told where he could put his apparatus. 'Half an hour, doing nothing? You try it, sunshine.'

What had really surprised him was the fact that no one had suggested, rightly, that he was talking complete and utter nonsense. He knew that if he were to widen his field of operations he was dangerously likely to run up against people who knew as much about Hertzian waves as he did, or more than he did. And that brought on again his recurring guilt at deceiving these good trusting people.

At least he wasn't charging them for the services of his apparatus. Considering the outrageous claims made on behalf of powders and pills, tinctures, liniments, therapeutic machines and miraculous cleaning products, he could be making a small fortune out of the Electric Telepath. There was no need to bring God into it; he could peddle the thing from door to door, gulling people into believing that with a Briggs patent Electric Telepath machine they would be able to communicate with each other without oral speech or the written word. Really unscrupulous persons would not even bother to make a genuine apparatus. They would, in exchange for substantial sums, palm off on their dupes useless imitations.

And yet he could advertise it with impunity; he really could patent it. Faraday had refused to patent anything. Knowledge should be freely available to all, Faraday had thought.

The Elders were already discussing the next experiment.

'May I suggest,' Elijah suggested, 'that this time a passage is chosen that is less, er, opaque?'

'Why, Elijah, you know how it was chosen,' Father said. 'Not by human agency.'

'No, of course not,' Elijah agreed, 'but I got the

impression that the strongest receivers even were confused. No one was familiar with that passage. I rather think they feared that what they were receiving had nothing to do with the still small voice and after that they attended less carefully. 'I mean, dragons, Pharaoh, rivers . . . the images' – good word – 'could have been coming from anywhere.'

'Images,' Elder Brayfield mused. 'Do you think that that is what is received? Images . . . pictures. I propose that in the next experiment, at least one of us should be a subject.'

Elijah could not decide if he liked the idea or not. Brayfield was a retired schoolmaster. He showed no signs of being better educated than his pupils, many of whom were at large around the Trident, but he fancied himself as a man of learning. Was he also secretly a sceptic, not in the matter of religion, obviously, but in the matter of science. The fact that the Electric Telepath was not science was of no consequence. He, Elijah, would have no influence over what Elder Brayfield received. He might, like everyone else involved, convince himself that he had experienced something – roses, laudanum, a headache – or he might denounce the whole business as an error. No one would call it a fraud, that idea would never enter their innocent minds – his conscience kicked again – but if nothing happened to Elder Brayfield he would probably conclude that nothing had happened to anyone else.

He would be right.

Elijah wished passionately now that he could somehow call the whole thing off. At least he might be able to exploit the obvious failure to achieve anything substantial.

The apparatus was saved, Father's reputation was saved and so was his, so far as he had one. He had conducted an experiment and it had failed. It could be called an honourable failure. Perhaps he could imply to his subjects, when he interviewed them afterwards, that this time there had been no effect. Perhaps he might voice his own doubts, declaring that the results were too ambiguous, but would the Elders take any notice? They wanted to believe. And was it not part of their creed, of any creed, that anything they believed in had to be true?

Twelve

He sat in the laboratory and wrote up his record of the second experiment in the quasi-biblical prose he had devised for the annals of the Electric Telepath.

> There were gathered together the Elders of the Congregation of Mount Horeb. And the Lord guided Elder Campion to choose the passage of Scripture that should be conveyed by the Apparatus to the faithful who had undertaken to hearken unto it. And the passage of Scripture was this:

And here he could have wept. Elder Campion had opened the Bible at the end of the Gospel according to St Luke, or the beginning of the Gospel according to St John. Elijah, seeing it upside down, recognized the layout of the pages at once and prayed, 'Oh, no, not that,' but inexorably Elder Campion's blunt stub of a finger had descended on chapter 1, verse 1.

Why should Elijah's prayer be answered? His every action mocked the sacred words; why should God care how he felt about this particular verse: 'In the beginning was the Word, and the Word was with God, and the Word was God'? He had always thought them the most beautiful lines in the whole book, it was a perfect passage to meditate upon, but he could scarcely bring himself to discharge the jars, to excite the wave, to dishonour the words with his miserable deception. And now he had to set out again, round the Trident, fifteen houses this time, trying to find out what people thought they had received. And if they had received nothing it would make no difference because, he knew now, they would demand to try again.

This had nothing to do with the still small voice, everything to do with novelty. It was as bad as claiming to speak with spirits, as useless as thought reading, the parlour trick that Gunnings had called it. They were like an illusionist's audience, eager to be duped, eager to be called up on stage to be duped personally and publicly in front of everyone else. And he must call on them all: Mrs Gilstrap, Jack Morrell, Miss Gallow, the Aubreys; and Lily.

Could he confide in Lily? And if he did would she be shocked, disgusted, amused, contemptuous? He ached to know whether she had pretended to get the message simply to please him – well, yes, obviously she must have done, since she *hadn't* got the message – but did she wish to seem blessed in his eyes or did she just want him to go away happy?

He confided in Gunnings, who shrugged.

'Well, make up your mind. Do you want them to think it works or don't you?'

'But they *do* think it works, and I know it doesn't.'

'Then you'll have to make sure it doesn't, won't you? Let everyone know it's an utter failure. That shouldn't be hard – for you.'

There was something in his friend's voice that Elijah had never heard before: scorn.

He was entirely unprepared for what happened next. He had planned to call first at the houses on the northern side of the Trident, between Trimley Road and Holloway Hill, to get the Gilstraps out of the way, cravenly leaving the Aubreys till last, or perhaps next to last, saving Lily as a final consolation when the ghastly task was over.

When he arrived at the Gilstraps' he was aware of excited faces watching for him under the lace curtains of The Vista. Three heads, the multitudinous teeth of Honoria, Gladys and Helen; like Cerberus, he thought bitterly, guarding the gates of Hades. When he rang the bell he heard a stampede of hooves rushing to open the door and the trio stood there beaming, having forestalled the Strict and Particular Baptist, who was skulking by the green baize door, balked of her chance to despise him face to face.

'Come in, quick, quick!' Honoria said, almost grabbing him.

'Put him down Nonnie, I saw him first,' Gladys shrieked. Helen slammed the door as if to cut off his retreat. She *was* cutting off his retreat: he found himself being hustled towards the sitting room. This was worse than the tittering and sly glances, worse than Horace's smirk – where *was* Horace? Oh God, there he stood, poised behind his mother in a protective attitude, one hand on her shoulder, one hand thrust into his jacket as if posing for a photograph. Mrs Gilstrap was seated on the gorilla chair, her skirts spread over the low arms like drapery.

'Tell him, tell him, Ma,' Helen squealed.

'Do sit down, Mr Briggs,' Mrs Gilstrap said. Horace inclined his head slightly, seconding the invitation.

Elijah did not want to sit. It was the first time he had encountered so many Gilstraps standing up; how big they were. He seemed to be shrinking where he stood, but he had no choice. Honoria half dragged, half shoved him on to the sofa, unaware of what her mother kept among the cushions. He felt something hard connect with his hip bone.

'It was quite wonderful,' Mrs Gilstrap began, but the shrill exclamations of her daughters drowned her voice.

'We all heard it!'

'We all sat and listened for the still small voice!'

'Seven thirty, we all sat down in here and held hands—'

They'd been holding a séance.

'And for, oh, ten minutes, we didn't get anything and then – and then—'

'Go on, Nonnie, tell him.'

'No, let Mother.'

'It was quite wonderful,' Mrs Gilstrap said tranquilly, as though she had not been interrupted. 'We were all sitting perfectly still. I had even had the canary bird moved to the dining room—'

'I think that was a mistake, Mother.' It was the first time that Elijah had heard Horace speak. It afforded him a moment of savage satisfaction. Horace's voice had not broken. 'They carry disease.'

'Perfectly still,' Mrs Gilstrap resumed. 'And then, quite suddenly, Honoria said, "The Word."'

'What word?' Elijah asked.

'Oh, don't be silly,' Honoria butted in. 'That's what came to me, the still small voice, it was talking about the Word.'

'And then I got "God",' Gladys cried, as if she had been dealt a good hand at whist. 'And "beginning with God".' Not a good card, a good hand; a royal flush.

'And then it came to me,' Mrs Gilstrap said. 'The Gospel According to St John, chapter one, verse one: "In the beginning was the Word, and the Word was with God and the Word was God. The same was in the beginning with God. All things were made by him; and without him was not anything made that was made."'

This was far in excess of what had been transmitted, since Elder Campion had stopped at verse 1.

'Were we right?' Helen demanded, in her escalating squeak. 'Did we guess right? Did we get it?'

'Hush, Nelly. It isn't a game,' Mrs Gilstrap said mildly. 'They're so excited, Mr Briggs. Do tell us, did we receive the message?'

'Yes,' Elijah said, weakly. 'Yes you did. Absolutely. St John one, verse one, that was what I transmitted.'

'So you can tell your father that we have received the still small voice and the Electric Telepath is working,' Mrs Gilstrap said.

Elijah's own voice seemed to him to be very faint and coming from far away.

'And shall you be attending the chapel?' He got it out

somehow. That, after all, was the purpose of listening for the still small voice.

'We'll have to see about that,' Mrs Gilstrap said, under cover of another tumult of delighted laughter. He was not sure of the reason for the laughter or for the delight. 'We usually go to St Asaph's and I had intended to attend the new church in Trimley Road.'

'Wait till they get a roof on it,' Gladys said pertly.

'Shut up, Ga-ga,' Horace piped. Ga-ga! It was getting worse by the second. How was Horace known to his nearest and dearest? Horsy? Ha-ha?

'But do remember me to your dear father. I shall be following the fortunes of your clever machine *closely* in future.'

As he left, from across the hall the exiled canary gave a shrill whistle of derision.

At the gate he turned left and went on up the hill, past Roper's building plots, the scaffolding and stacks of new bricks standing around the foundations of the houses where the Gilstraps' future neighbours would settle.

He knew they had watched him leave, but this way he was immediately out of their range. Let them wonder where he was going, he did not know himself. Holloway Hill, the ancient drovers' road, was still scarcely more than a rutted track here, long since stripped of the double hedgerow that had given it its name. Fields lay on both sides, ploughed and wintry. He sat on a stile in the lee of a leafless beech hanger and stared down over the Trident, seeing nothing.

How had they done it?

They had cheated, that much was evident; not poor silly fuddled Mrs Gilstrap but the girls, with or without the connivance of Horace.

Honoria, Nonnie, had started it with 'the Word', and Ga-ga had followed with 'beginning with God' and after that their mother, unconsciously putting the two together, as anyone would who knew her scriptures, had come up with the whole quotation, not just the transmitted first verse but 2 and 3 with it; that was the giveaway. No one, even after his most overt promptings, had followed Ezekiel 29, verse 3, with Ezekiel 29, verse 4, but Mrs Gilstrap had received more than she had been sent.

Perhaps she had simply assumed that she was meant to get the rest of the passage. If Nelly hadn't interrupted she might have reeled off the whole chapter.

How had they known? Far from reinforcing his belief in the transmission of thought it made him more than ever sure that it was impossible, particularly impossible utilizing the medium of the electromagnetic wave. And they had been quite certain that they had got it right.

That was it. Nelly had spoken of guessing, but it had been no guess. Someone had told Nonnie Gilstrap, or Ga-ga, or Nelly, that the passage transmitted had been St John, chapter 1, verse 1.

No. It couldn't have happened afterwards; they had known already.

Assuming Mrs Gilstrap to be honest, and he was sure that she was, she and her family had sat down and earnestly listened for the still small voice last Friday evening at 7.30. At 7.30 Elijah and the Elders had been assembled in the committee room, around the apparatus, and as Elder Bland's repeater had announced the half hour, Elder Campion, divinely guided, had opened his Bible and placed his finger on the chosen passage. Until that very second no one had known what the passage would be except, presumably, the Lord. No one, that was, except . . .

He could not believe that he was thinking what he was thinking. Elder Campion was no less devout than his brethren; he was, like the others, a recognized pillar of probity . . . but no one except Elder Campion *could* have known in advance. Elijah relived the scene in the committee room. He had watched the Bible fall open, apparently at random, but he knew from experience that books could fall open reliably at certain pages, and Elder Campion had been using his own Bible. And St John's Gospel began two thirds of the way down the left-hand page. He saw it all again, and relived the horror, as Elder Campion's finger descended upon verse 1.

He *must* have decided in advance and, more than that, communicated the decision to someone. Elijah could not quite imagine Elder Campion in a giggling huddle with Nonnie Gilstrap but now he was certain; somehow the choice of verse to be transmitted had been made ahead of the experiment and told to an interested party.

But why? Why should Elder Campion be so anxious for the experiment to succeed; and who else had he told?

From between two clouds a shaft of sunlight fell on the Trident, particularly on the eastern end of the Trident, on the nearer stretch of Ryecart Road, and the garden of 216. A tiny figure, a woman, was crossing the lawn between two bare fruit trees. Was it Lily? Was it Maggie? Ought he to go down now and find out what Lily had received that night? Or should he face the other suspects – *subjects* – first? How could he confront Elder Campion with what he knew; and how much did he know?

Was Elder Campion desperate for the experiment to work because he longed for proof (o faithless one) of the still small voice, or had he another reason? It couldn't be sheer devilment, surely; not in an Elder of the Congregation of Mount Horeb.

As he was engaged in collecting results of the experiment he was excused the weekly missions rota, which meant that he might choose the time of his call on the Aubreys. He could spy on their movements from the upstairs landing window and when he was sure that at least one William was off the premises he could slip across. Mrs Aubrey was occasionally seen in the street, marching as to war even if she were only going shopping, umbrella gripped like a cudgel and an unpleasant black bonnet that resembled a fillet of turbot perched on her hair-do. On all his visits he had never had occasion to speak to her; she was an unseen malignancy behind closed door, presumably the source of the shrieks.

So he would leave the Aubreys till tomorrow. No one, he surmised, would have tried to nobble *them*.

He slid from the stile, crossed the track and walked down over the green corduroy of winter wheat towards the brickworks, where he could cut through to The Crescent. He was aware of the Gilstrap residence on its eminence, glimpsed at intervals between the semi-detached villas, but the sisters must have left the window by now. In case they hadn't, he tried to assume a carefree air, head up, shoulders back, but his heart was not in it. He was no longer looking forward to seeing Lily; in truth, he was beginning to dread it.

An hour ago he had been telling himself that this time, when it became obvious that she had received nothing, he would confess, take her into his confidence, throw himself on her mercy. But now he had to face the possibility that she would tell him, yes, she had heard the still small voice and blithely recite the opening versus of St John's Gospel. How could he then look her in the eye and ask outright, 'Who told you?'

The footpath joined what had been Brickworks Lane and was now The Crescent. As he entered the curve, where the pavement ran alongside the Ropers' garden wall, a door in the wall opened and Lily herself stepped out. She had her back to him but his already-churning brain reminded him that the upper windows of 216 must command a view of the hillside he had just crossed. If it had been Lily he had seen in the garden, might she not also have seen him sitting on the stile? But the female figure crossing the lawn had been too distant to identify; she could never have identified him unless she had watched him crossing the fields. Could it be coincidence that she had come out of the side gate at the moment he happened to be approaching it? After the experiment she must be expecting him to call; perhaps she could not wait. He quickened his pace.

'Miss Roper! Lily!'

She gave a little start and turned. She was not dressed for the street and she was carrying a Sussex trug and a pair of secateurs.

'Elijah! What must you think of me looking like this out of doors?'

She looked enchanting.

'You look . . . just right, Lily.'

'I'm gardening – I didn't want to tread mud through the house so I came round this way. What are you doing here?'

She must mean, 'What are you doing in The Crescent, where none of the houses is yet occupied?' Perhaps she hadn't seen him on the footpath.

'I was coming to see you,' he said.

'I wish I'd known, I wouldn't have chosen to let you see me in this state.'

She was wearing a headscarf knotted at the nape of her neck, a sacking apron with deep pockets, and wooden shoes. She reminded him of a beautiful peasant girl in a fairy tail. Ogres, envious stepsisters, vengeful witches waited on the far side of the wall.

'What are you pruning?'

'Oh, that's all done. Father likes to take care of the fruit trees. I'm just cutting things back before it gets really cold and wet.'

How much colder and wetter could that be? he wondered. The autumn rains were already given way to hard frosts.

'I suppose you wouldn't like to hold the trug for me – unless you're in a frightful hurry?'

Had she forgotten the Electric Telepath? He obediently took the trug, since she was offering it to him, and followed her round to the front garden, where he stood in silence, holding out the trug, while she paced pensively along the borders, snipping off the heads of the last chrysanthemums and the few pallid roses that clung to the trellis by the porch. She still did not speak and he stared unseeing into the dark recesses of the parlour beyond the window, where a lusher specimen of an aspidistra than their own stood on the sill. He was horribly shocked when he saw movement and Maggie's grim face looking back at him. She was assiduously dusting the leaves of the aspidistra in a manner suggesting that this was a cover for her vigil.

At last Lily, still bending over a chrysanthemum and tweaking out its petals as if she were pulling the wings off a fly, said, 'Well, aren't you going to ask me?'

He temporized. 'Ask you what?'

'Oh, Elijah, *you* know. And I've been dying to tell you. The still small voice.'

He swallowed. 'I was awfully afraid you might not have got it, this time.'

'Oh, but I did. And it was as clear as anything.' She turned to face him, smiling innocently. He tried to meet her eyes but Maggie was still at work on the aspidistra. '"In the beginning was the Word."'

'You heard that?'

Her smile faltered. 'Wasn't that right? I was so sure—'

'Yes,' he said miserably, 'that was it.'

'Of course, I didn't actually *hear* it, the same as last time. It just came to me as I sat there listening. I'd love to see your magnetrical apparatus sometime, Elijah. It must be fascinating.'

Thirteen

Somehow he got away, mumbling about others to see, and she quite understood.

'But we'll meet again soon, won't we?' She waved goodbye to him over the gate and turned back to her dead-heading, but when he looked round again from the corner of Trimley Road, he saw her scooting back along the pavement to the side gate. Her work was done. She *had* intercepted him, not because she longed for his company but because she had information to deliver.

He crossed the street to Jack Morrell's forge, where Jack was bent over a carthorse's hairy hoof. Elijah recognized the horse; it was the Aubreys' animal. The horse, he thought, recognized him and bared its teeth, and then he saw William Senior lounging in the shadows.

'Got it this time!' William bellowed, only ten feet away but congenitally unable to lower his voice from a shout.

Elijah pretended not to hear. Jack was looking at him quizzically, the hoof, the size of a soup plate, between his knees.

'I've come about the Electric Telepath experiment,' Elijah said, raising his voice for Jack's benefit but trying not to compete with William. 'Thursday night. Did you hear anything?'

'Worms,' Jack said.

'Worms?'

'Something about worms. It was dragons last time, wasn't it?'

'Wasn't worms,' William Senior bawled. 'It was the Word. "In the beginning was the Word." In the beginning was the worm – oh, that's a good 'un.'

Elijah had to acknowledge him now. 'Yes, that's right, Mr Aubrey. The Word. Did anyone else hear anything?'

'We all heard it. Once we'd worked out what it was, we got it loud and clear,' William said.

Elijah understood what he had meant by the time he reached his own front door. Even while he, in all innocence, in all ignorance, had gone from subject to subject, enjoining them to set aside a few moments to listen for the still small voice, someone else had been making it clear that they should be listening for the Word.

'The word?' they would have said. 'What word?'

'The Word of God, like, "In the beginning",' they would have been told.

And that, naturally, was exactly what they had heard, except for deaf Jack Morrell.

Being deaf ought to have no effect upon the still small voice, that was the whole point of it; the still small voice spoke without sound. Who was it who had stood in the smithy, fruitlessly yelling, 'Listen for the Word, the *Word*, the WORD!' at Jack. Was it the same person who had got at Nonnie Gilstrap, dropped heavy hints to Lily and the Aubreys? Who, and even more troubling, why? He simply could not see Elder Campion undertaking it, and only Campion could have been at the back of it. Who was his cat's paw?

It came to him later. Who could it be but Charlie? *Charlie?*

Charlie Campion whom Maggie had once sent packing? She hadn't sent him packing this time.

By Tuesday, the date of the next meeting of the newly-formed Electric Telepath Committee, he thought he had the evidence he needed, but what was he to do with it? Father was not in for supper and it was Abigail's turn to say Grace. Pale and big-eyed, her head level with the teapot on its trivet, she stood and recited: 'May the Lord relieve necessity in others and may we ourselves give thanks that we are not in want or penury. Amen.'

Elijah, looking down at her, thought how wretchedly undersized she was, how wan. It was not that Agnes did not feed her – they were all, always, fairly served at table – but how could she grow when she never went out, never ran about, never played with other kids, got her only exercise throwing an India-rubber ball at the strip of wall at the end of the garden? The rest of the time she was hunched over Mangnall's *Questions* and those everlasting psalms, trying to catch up with the insufferable Ezra, two years younger.

I'll buy her a hoop for Christmas! he thought, and the picture of Abigail racing down the long slope of Ryecart Road, hair streaming, boots clattering, the hoop bowling beside her, made him smile.

The Congregation of Mount Horeb could not be said to celebrate Christmas, it smacked too much of worldly pleasures, although the exchange of small gifts of a devotional nature was countenanced. But no one could grudge a little girl her hoop. Ezra, rot him, should have an illuminated text to hang above the bed: *Though I speak with the tongues of men and of angels, and have not charity, I am become as sounding brass, or a tinkling cymbal.*

'Amen. What are you grinning about?' Agnes said as they sat down.

'I was looking forward to this evening,' Elijah lied. 'Where's Dad?'

'He had to see some of the other Elders before the meeting,' Agnes said. 'I'll put out some cold pie and pickles for when he gets back afterwards – and don't you go eating them, you're having your supper now.'

'Who's he seeing?' Elijah asked, thinking that there must be other ways of cooking cabbage than boiling it to death like a heretic and crushing the life's blood out of it, leaving it flaccid, steaming and bitter. Then Agnes's words got through to him. 'Why?'

'How should I know? It's none of our business, is it? If he wants to tell you about it, he will.'

Elijah wondered about that. When it was time for pudding he said, 'Aggie, if we do another experiment with the Electric Telepath, would you take part?'

'No,' Agnes said calmly, without even having to think about it. 'It's dangerous.'

'How can it be dangerous? You wouldn't be anywhere near it. It's not even dangerous if you *are* near it.'

'Electric rays – how do we know what they're doing, where they're going, getting into people's heads?'

'Electromagnetic waves. We do know where they go, they go everywhere.'

'Then it's very irresponsible of you to be making them.'

'But they're everywhere anyway. Light is an electromagnetic wave. They don't need me to make them.'

'But you're using them,' Agnes said. 'You may say you are using them to carry the still small voice, but if they can be used by God they can be used by Satan too. *One* spoonful of jam in the tapioca, Abby. You don't see Ezra taking two, do you?'

No, no one *saw* Ezra taking two, but looking at his brother's plate of milk pudding, Elijah could tell that he had.

On his way round to the chapel he remembered that Elder Brayfield had volunteered to be a subject this time. Elijah had not put him on the list since he had no intention of calling on him to enquire about the result, knowing that he would announce it anyway, in public. He became very curious to know what Elder Brayfield had received.

When he went into the committee room the Elders were drinking tea. They looked benignly upon Elijah but did not offer him any. Instead they instantly put their cups down on the side table and settled into their chairs, indicating that he should join them.

'So, young Briggs, tell us the results,' Elder Foregate said, when Elijah had sat down and said nothing. 'We are all ears.'

Elijah took out the list. 'Of all subjects consulted, eight were uncertain of having received anything at all.' He included Jack Morrell in the eight but as he spoke he noticed that although the list comprised households, to correspond with the map, two of those households, the Gilstraps and the Aubreys, had brought the number of confirmations up from seven to sixteen; from just under half to over two thirds, assuming that Elder Brayfield had heard what he was meant to hear.

'That is most encouraging,' Elder Campion said as the results were read out, and Elijah could not look at him.

'I haven't included Elder Brayfield,' he said. 'What did you receive, sir?'

Elder Brayfield arose. 'As you will recall,' he announced, 'I absented myself from the transmission in order to act as a receiver. I made every preparation for uninterrupted contemplation, instructed my wife and the girl to refrain from conversation even in the next room. I sat in silence and gave all my attention to the still small voice. I regret to say' – and Elder Brayfield neither looked nor sounded regretful – 'that I heard nothing.'

Oh, incorruptible Elder Brayfield . . . or had no one bothered to corrupt him? Elder Campion, working through the medium of Charlie, must have known from the start that Brayfield was a poor lookout. Elder Brayfield's head was bent; Elijah could not look him in the eye, but all the same he knew what he was thinking. He was positively rejoicing in the fact that he had not received the message, not least because he had not expected to; was convinced moreover that it would be impossible to receive it via the Electric Telepath. Elijah could have hugged the old beast.

Little murmurings of sympathy came from his fellow Elders. Brayfield sat down. Campion arose.

'Well,' he said, 'in spite of that, I think we have sufficiently encouraging results to lay before Elder Hullard. If you are agreeable I will draft a letter to him tonight.'

The sounds of sympathy gave way to vigorous assent. Elder Brayfield alone sat mute and, it seemed to Elijah, who also had nothing to say, mutinous. Who was Elder Hullard and what had he to do with the Electric Telepath? Elijah felt the first stirrings of panic. While the experiments involved only the Trident and the Elders of the Cater Street chapel, the whole ridiculous business could be contained, but by the sound of it they were planning to extend operations to other congregations.

What was Father's part in all this? He could not believe that Father was a party to whatever Elder Campion was up to: Father, who could never have committed an act of deception in his life.

But did Campion regard what he was doing as deception? From his investigations in library and reading room Elijah had perceived that more than one man of science in the past had claimed results that could not be proven, which was excusable in matters of faith, but not of physics. He could understand that Campion might be eager to believe in the Electric Telepath – so was Father; so were they all except Elder Brayfield – but why so anxious that he was prepared to salt the mine, as it were?

'Don't forget to enter your findings in the book,' Elder Campion said.

'And on the map,' Father added.

'When I hear from Elder Hullard,' Campion went on, 'we shall conduct a third experiment. I think we are all agreed on that?'

Yes, they were all agreed, except for Elder Brayfield. Elijah longed for a private word with Elder Brayfield but feared to approach him. Who, after all, had started this nonsense? Brayfield would ask him.

'Perhaps you could do that now,' Father said.

'Do what?'

'Add the names to the map. While we have the place heated it would be a sin to waste it.' The heat had come from the non-extinguished oil stove in the corner, little of it and odoriferous. As the Elders put on their coats and departed, Elijah took down the map in its frame and fetched his ink and mapping pens from the book cupboard.

How happy he had been in that cupboard, his laboratory, pursuing something real, tangible, that might lead to wonderful discoveries. Goodbye to all that.

Downstairs he found his father in hat and coat, ready to leave but waiting for him.

'It seems only fair to tell you,' Elder Briggs said, as Elijah sat down and opened the ink bottle, 'that we have informed Headquarters of your apparatus. Elder Hullard of the Halifax Congregation has expressed warm interest in our findings. Elder Campion has every confidence that if the next experiment is as successful as this one, the Halifax Congregation may be prepared to invest in its development.'

'Invest?'

'Through your experiments, Elijah, we have been vouchsafed a wondrous means to spread the word of the still small voice.'

'Isn't it too soon to tell?' Elijah said, wanly. 'After only two experiments?'

'I think we may count the last one as a resounding success,' Elder Briggs said. 'What we propose to do next time is to choose different subjects. Elder Campion suggests that you should concentrate on refining the apparatus while he approaches the subjects.'

'*Does* he?' Elijah said. Now he knew he had the proof he needed. He was on the verge of saying, 'Father, I think he's been doing that already,' but how could he tell the Old Man that Elder Campion, his trusted friend and colleague, was fiddling the results? Father would never believe him.

He finished writing in the names, blotted them and rehung the map on the wall, where it mocked him; the newly ruled red lines still glistening, the red halo around the chapel, the names of those impressionable subjects. All that effort and craftsmanship gone into bearing witness to a deception, testimony to his modest scientific curiosity that had been distorted to serve that deception – no, to be the instrument of that deception. And whose fault was that?

As they walked home together in the frosty dark he said, 'Father, a real test of the apparatus would be to ask people who hadn't *been* listening for the still small voice.'

'How do you mean?' Elder Briggs said. 'That is what

Elder Campion has in mind, to find subjects who are new to the experiment.'

'That's not what I meant,' Elijah said. 'If the still small voice is being carried, it is by the electromagnetic wave which I produce by discharging the Leyden jars. That wave does not go in a single straight line to each of those houses, it goes everywhere, not just to people who are listening for it.'

'That is even more wonderful!' Elder Briggs said. 'We can carry the still small voice even to people who do not want to hear it, to those who would close their ears to it.'

Henry Walker? Elijah could imagine what Henry would say if he thought that people were trying to get ideas into his head without his knowledge. 'Isn't that cheating, Dad? Isn't man endowed with free will to choose whether he listens or not?'

'Mysterious are the ways of the Lord,' Elder Briggs said, fervently. And the ways of Elder Campion, Elijah thought. 'You told us yourself, electromagnetism is the work of His hand. Now that we have discovered its existence He will guide our use of it.'

Hearing his own words turned against him, Elijah struggled for an answer. You could advance the same argument in the defence of dynamite, which had been intended for blasting rock before other uses had been found for it. Had God intended saltpetre to be a constituent of gunpowder, or iron to be made into cannonballs? What was to stop unscrupulous men embedding their own messages in the words of the still small voice? *Thus saith the Lord: use only Mattison's*

Pectoral Liniment. Two shillings a box. Trust no other.

He was saved from having to answer by a violent altercation on the far side of the road. Almost since they had left the chapel he had been aware of shouting somewhere in the vicinity, muffled by distance but coming closer. As they rounded the corner into Ryecart Road they saw the source of it. A gang of youths and boys was surrounding two roaring, flailing men, yelling encouragement. There was a streetlamp on the corner, throwing enough light to expose the combatants as Williams Senior and Junior, conducting what had obviously been a running battle that was now severely impeded by the ring of spectators. The dog was in there too, by the sound of it, snarling and growling impartially.

'I must intervene,' Elder Briggs said, mindful of his duty as a spiritual leader and a concerned citizen. 'This is a dreadful spectacle.'

He started across the road. Elijah seized his coat sleeve and tried to drag him away. 'No, Dad, don't get into that. It won't do any good.' Small skirmishes were breaking out in sympathy around the fringes of the mob.

'I cannot pass by on the other side!' Elder Briggs cried, struggling to free himself from Elijah, who was intent on making him do just that. He saw sticks and bottles in the clenched fists: the Old Man might be laid out, even mortally hurt. Aware that his own tussle mirrored the father-and-son dispute on the opposite pavement, he hung on desperately, hoping that none of the crowd would notice them, scent the prospect of another fight and come over to enjoy it. Then a whistle was heard farther down the street, someone shouted, '*Rozzers!*' and like black beetles disturbed by sudden light the whole boiling melted into the darkness and the Aubreys, having reached their gates, stumbled through the wicket. It slammed behind them, almost cutting the dog in two as it scrambled through urgently at their heels, but did not contain the thumps and curses that contained on the other side. By the time the thudding feet of the dispersing mob had given way to the approaching boots of a police constable, the street was deserted except for Elder Briggs and Elijah, who were by now at their own front door.

The policeman, swinging his bull's-eye round, saw them on the step, and thinking that they had come out in response to the disturbance, called across reassuringly.

'Evening, Mr Briggs. Nothing to worry about, a street fight, all over now,' but from force of habit he opened the Aubreys' wicket and stepped inside.

In the hall they found Agnes with a poker guarding the foot of the stairs like Horatius keeping the bridge in the brave days of old. Ezra and Abby, in nightgowns, crouched at the top, hands clasped.

'We were praying to be delivered,' Ezra said.

'It was only the Aubreys,' Elijah told them. 'All quiet now, nothing to worry about, there's a constable over there.'

Agnes looked at him reproachfully, as though he had been out of the house by choice, engaged in frivolous pursuits in dereliction of his duty to the family.

'It's been going on all evening, on and off.'

'There, there, I said we should be back by half past eight

and we are,' Father said. 'Go to bed, children, we are in God's hands.'

Elijah was helping him off with his coat. He looked round. 'You should not have tried to restrain me, Elijah. We cannot turn aside from such evils in our streets.'

'No, Father, but there must have been thirty of them out there. You could have done no good and you might have been hurt. God knows you were willing,' he said consolingly.

'I must pray for those unhappy fellows,' Father said, and toddled towards his study.

It seemed not to have occurred to him, Elijah thought, that if the Aubreys had heard the still small voice it had failed signally to move them. At all events, the awkward debate about the Electric Telepath had been suspended. He wished he could forget about it altogether but one word continued to haunt him: *invest*. Elder Hullard of Halifax Headquarters was considering investing in the wretched apparatus.

Investing what? Time? Energy? To what end did he wish to invest; to spread the still small voice – or did he have in mind a more literal investment: capital? And what kind of a return would he expect on his investment?

Fourteen

He had abandoned the Trimley Road reading room for the Town Hall library, where Father thought he had been working all along. That this was one deception he was no longer practising on the Old Man did nothing to ease his conscience. Where was it all going? Where was it all going to end? He was past the point where he could face the Elders and admit that the whole business was a colossal sell, because he was certain that Elder Campion knew perfectly well it was exactly that and was preparing to make it even more colossal.

Love of money is the root of all evil, he transmitted silently. Are you getting that, you old fraud? Go on, read my thoughts.

On the other side of the table Gunnings sat, head bowed over the *Illustrated London News*. They had not come to the library together; it was a long while since they had done anything together apart from share a desk in the form room at roll call before going their separate ways to lessons, Gunnings on the Classics side, Elijah to Moderns. That had never been a problem before, why should it be one now? They had always come together again after school: Elijah had helped Gunnings develop his plates; Gunnings had helped Elijah build the apparatus. Gunnings had never sneered at the Horebites, Elijah had never tried to convert Gunnings; they'd agreed to differ.

But now the difference yawned between them and Elijah no longer knew how to bridge it.

He had longed to tell Gunnings about Elder Campion's activities – he desperately needed an ally – but every time he was on the point of saying something he remembered the Gilstrap connection. He felt he was already providing the Gilstraps with enough innocent merriment without Gunnings adding to it. Worse, he suspected that Gunnings actively disapproved of what he was doing, Gunnings who had always appeared so easy-going about matters of right and wrong.

If only there were someone Elijah *could* tell. The Roman Catholics, he believed, were able to confess – confess *anything* – to a priest, and the priest would set them a penance and they would be forgiven. Once that would have meant walking to Rome barefoot or with stones in their shoes. Now, he understood, it was the saying of certain prayers many times, which were efficacious if you were heartily sorry; and he was heartily sorry, but there was no such absolution available to the Congregation of Mount Horeb. He was left alone with his conscience and the still small voice.

When Gunnings saw him come into the library he nodded affably and shifted his books to make room at the table, but he did not whisper jokes or pass notes as he would have done once, and not long after Elijah had sat down Gunnings had gathered his things together and left, with another nod. No hard feelings; no feelings at all.

There was nothing to keep Elijah in the library. Since it was for the advancement of all and not just the working man it stocked wider reading matter, but there were far fewer scientific and engineering journals, not even the *Digest*. And what was the use of reading them anyway? Elijah asked himself. None of it was any use, he was never going to escape, he was trapped. He would spend the rest of his life half-educated, unqualified, urging people to listen for the still small voice while Elder Campion perpetrated a cynical fraud on people who knew so little, and resisted knowing more, that they would believe anything. What was his thirst for knowledge in the face of such an almighty thirst for ignorance?

The way out of the library was through the lofty tile-and-mosaic vestibule of the Town Hall, past the corridor to the town museum with its dusty cases of butterfly collections, beetle collections, minerals and small forlorn fossils. In London was the British Museum, one of the wonders of the modern world, and he had never seen it. He never would see it. He had never been to London and he never would go. Father had moved from Gloucester to Lembridge at the age of eighteen and had never left it. Elijah might be there for life.

On his way home up Trimley Road he thought he recognized the figure of Charlie Campion slipping around the corner by the pillar box at the end of Cater Street.

He did not often see Charlie away from the chapel. During the day he was at work in the fish shop, the rest of the time he was trotting around in his father's wake, much as Elijah had once trotted around behind Elder Briggs. Unlike Elijah, Charlie was rarely trusted to do missionary work unaccompanied so Elijah was surprised to see him out on his own, but the surprise swiftly gave way to the thought that this might be the confirmation of his suspicions.

He crossed the road and, keeping to the shadows, fell in twenty yards or so behind Charlie. When Charlie turned in at a gateway he noted the number of the house. The Horebites kept a record of their Congregants; it would be easy to check up on who Charlie was visiting, and why.

For his suspicions were base. In preparation for the third experiment everything had been taken out of his hands except for the actual transmission of the wave. They could hardly take the apparatus away from him, he reflected. None of them knew how it worked and they were all, Campion included, slightly in awe of it.

He allowed himself to catch up with his quarry just as Charlie was approaching the chapel. He sprinted a step or two and brought his hand down on Charlie's shoulder. Charlie jumped, but only, he thought, with surprise, not guilt. Charlie's face was guileless when Elijah confronted him.

'About the Lord's work?' Elijah said, cheerily.

'Oh – hullo, Briggs. Thought you were going to garrotte me,' Charlie said. 'Yes, just telling people about that thing of Dad's.'

'What thing's that?' Elijah said, equally guileless.

'I don't know; that electrical thing that spreads the still small voice.'

Dad's thing, was it? 'I've heard about that,' Elijah said. 'What do you tell them?'

'Oh, it's just the ones who are going to listen for it,' Charlie said. 'I have to tell them the day and the time, like.'

'And do you tell them what they're going to hear?'

'Can't,' Charlie said. 'See, no one knows that. That's why they have to listen. I just say, "You will know when the Lord speaks as he did to Samuel"; when Samuel thought it was Eli calling him and Eli said it wasn't. You know that bit.'

Elijah did know that bit, it was a favourite with the Congregation of Mount Horeb; everyone who attended the chapel would know that bit.

On Friday evening, when he brought the apparatus down to the Elders, he was aware of a difference in the atmosphere, in eagerness, almost excitement. Only Elder Brayfield held aloof, already sitting at the far end of the table.

When the others settled down Elijah took his place behind the apparatus and looked around, innocently enquiring.

'Who will choose the passage this time?' he asked, but he had already noticed that Elder Foregate held the Bible. So he's in on it too, Elijah thought. He stared hard at it, partly to see if he could detect a marker of some kind, partly in the hope of discomfiting Elder Foregate, but Foregate was already on his feet, eyes closed, head raised, and with glum resignation Elijah watched the pages open at 1 Samuel 3, and the finger drop unerringly on verse 10.

'"And the Lord came and stood, and called as at the

other times, Samuel, Samuel. Then Samuel answered, Speak, for thy servant heareth."'

And all over the Trident His servants were preparing to hear exactly that, for as soon as Charlie had called, Elijah knew, they would have had that very passage in their heads, might even have consulted their own Bibles to make sure that they would be listening, like Samuel, when the Lord spoke.

The Elders went through the usual rehearsal, although they must know it by heart, and then sat in contemplative silence as Elijah discharged the jars, excited the spark and sent his wave on its way. When they began to stir he said, with the same innocence, to Elder Campion, 'Sir, will you give me the list of subjects so that I can collect results as usual?'

'No need to bother about that,' Elder Campion said. 'I'll take care of it.'

I bet you will, Elijah thought.

'And will you tell me the results so that I can enter them in the book?'

'You worry about your apparatus,' Campion said. 'You may be required to build another one soon.' He exchanged a significant look with Elder Foregate. 'The book is in the cupboard, is it not? Perhaps you could bring it down when you put the apparatus away.'

'But the map—' His work of art. He could not bear the thought of Campion touching that.

'Not even the map,' Campion said. 'You have enough to do. Through you, Elijah, the Lord has shown us a new and wonderful means to reach the unenlightened. You should thank God upon your knees for having made you His instrument.'

Whose instrument?

'With your apparatus,' Foregate said, 'the Congregation of Mount Horeb will be able to convey the still small voice into the hearts and minds of those who are not even listening for it; those, in fact, whose hearts and minds have been corrupted by false prophets from other faiths.'

By whom he meant, presumably, the Wesleyans, Anglicans, Baptists, Roman Catholics. With the Electric Telepath, the newest technology, the Horebites could storm ahead of their less advanced rivals – at least, that was how Foregate and Campion would puff it to Headquarters. They must have been talking to Father, who had rejoiced in the thought that the SSV might reach even those who did not want to hear it. Was Father aware of the Campion-Foregate plan? Elijah could not believe that, but then he did not know what the plan was; still, he suspected that what the Elders had in mind was to patent the thing and make it available at a price to other congregations. And they had the brass to assume that there was nothing that he, the lowly instrument, submissive Congregant who had not even heard the SSV himself, could do about it.

And weren't they right?

Elijah watched the Elders leave with something like despair, and something like hatred for Elder Campion, who was studying his map, probably dreaming up fresh forgeries. He dismantled the apparatus and took it up to the book cupboard. He could no longer bear to call it his laboratory – the very word lent dignity to the whole preposterous farrago.

And what had he got out of it? He was no further forward with the real experiments he had hoped to conduct; quite the reverse: he had cemented himself even more firmly into the Congregation of Mount Horeb. I wouldn't have deceived them, he told himself. If the others hadn't been there that time when old Mother Elligot found the bomb, I'd have confessed to Father.

Would he have done? Oh what a tangled web . . .

Did anyone involved believe in what they were doing? How did they square it with their consciences? How did he square it with his? What did he believe in? The events of the last few weeks had left him with no faith in anything at all. How could God, the kindly, fair-minded God of the Horebites, allow his servants on earth to be taken in, especially by those of their own number. He had prayed for forgiveness, but he knew that he could not forgive himself. He had stopped supposing that anyone else could.

In the dark solitude of the cupboard he prayed, 'Let this last experiment be such a resounding failure that not even Elder Campion can pretend that it has worked,' but he no longer knew who he was praying to.

The fog was so thick in the streets that when he came out of the side entry of the chapel he could scarcely see the nearest lamp, and there, downwind of the gasworks, the roiling vapour was heavy with hydrogen sulphide, so thick that it deadened all sound, even his own hollow footfalls. In Milton Road he heard carts pass him invisibly.

Someone on the far side, attempting to whistle cheerfully, broke into a fit of coughing as if being strangled. Elijah buried his face in his muffler and tried not to breathe too deeply. He kept his left hand extended, touching the garden walls, counting gate posts; even so he misjudged the turning and found himself walking up someone's front path, alerting a nervous dog that bayed in the basement area.

When he reached the corner he wondered if he would be able to find even his own front door. So many of the houses in Ryecart Road being business premises, few had garden walls or gates. The silence thickened and seemed to hang particularly heavy over where he judged number 42 must be, the Aubreys' house and yard. He thought he detected the usual red glow above the gates, but there were no lights in the windows of the house, none of the customary cries and crashes, the baleful crackle of flames.

At home Agnes and the children were in a state of high excitement and all Father's efforts to calm them unsuccessful. There had been a terrible uproar earlier at the yard and then the police had arrived and there had been a great deal of coming and going, but they hadn't been able to see anything because of the fog. All Elijah could think was, if the experiment fails in spite of all their preparations, they'll put it down to the fog interfering with the wave. It was quite possible that atmospheric conditions really might affect electromagnetic waves, but Campion and Foregate were in no position to know that, one way or the other.

In the morning the fog was even thicker, the air yellow

and oily with coal smoke, oozing in at the letter box with the post, but the news got through it, all over the Trident, carried by word of mouth. During the previous evening a more than usually violent row had broken out among the Aubreys, which had ended with Mrs Aubrey opening their front door for the first time in living memory and running into the street, shrieking blue murder. She had not been seen since the police arrived, shortly afterwards. In fact, owing to the fog, no one had actually seen anything, but everyone knew what had happened.

The row began when William Junior had gone after William Senior with a six-foot angle iron; had climaxed with William Senior rounding on William Junior waving a coal shovel, pursuing him round the yard into the house and up the stairs, where William Junior had run into his grandfather, William the First, armed with a complete set of fire irons that he happened to have about him, turned at bay and, finding William Senior at his heels, kicked him down the stairs, where he lay stark dead and staring with his neck broken, head askew, while William Junior was dragged away by police constables crying, 'It was the voices! It was the machine! They put voices in my head, it was the voices made me do it!'

Fifteen

Since it had been generally assumed around the Trident that sooner or later one of the Aubreys would slaughter one of the others, nobody was particularly surprised, although everybody was shocked, or professed to be.

Sisters of Dorcas converged upon Mrs Aubrey and were beaten back by the grieving widow hefting a cast-iron frying pan as easily as a tennis racket. The Elders, having found the gates barred, met at the chapel by common consent. The Aubreys were, after all members of the Congregation; their troubles must afflict everyone alike. Elijah, who did not entirely agree, was summoned to join them and discovered that they had it in mind to employ the Electric Telepath to convey their prayers and sympathy to all concerned from a safe distance.

Considering what the Aubreys were alleging the Electric Telepath to have done, this struck him as verging on the suicidal; but, too dispirited to argue, he was in the committee room, charging the Leyden jars, when there came an ominous knocking at the front door of the chapel. Before any of them could go and answer it he heard it open and close again. The Elders were in the main body of the chapel and he thought he detected a collective *frisson*.

He went to the door and squinted round it. At the far end of the aisle stood a police officer.

He thought, They've come to arrest me. William has

told them my machine put the voices in his head and they believed him.

Elder Briggs stepped forward. 'Good evening, Sergeant.' Then he added faintly, 'Good evening, William,' and as the police sergeant stepped forward Elijah saw that behind him stood the dead man, William Aubrey Senior.

William Senior stopped where he was, flung up an arm and pointed directly at Elijah, standing in the doorway.

'There he is! That's him. He done it!'

Elijah's first instinct was to bolt back up the stairs to the cupboard and burrow through the air vent to make his escape via Henry Walker's shed and over garden walls until he reached the back of number 57 and sanctuary. He could not see the Elders from where he was standing but he sensed them all turning towards the doorway, slowly realizing whom William was pointing at. William advanced slowly, limping a little, past the police sergeant, still pointing, still shouting.

'Him and his machine, that's what done it, the machine, sending evil rays into people's heads while they sleep in their beds, setting them on to crime and felony. That's what done it, the electrical rays, going all over, creeping through our walls, filling our heads!'

Drawn as if by a magnet, Elijah walked towards the point of William's finger. The sergeant, apparently lost for words, stayed where he was.

'They're all at it!' William howled. 'Filling our heads with voices, that's what the boy heard, gentle as a lamb, that lad – ask his mother – never hurt a fly, you should see him handle frogs, and then along comes Briggs with his machine and his rays, filling our heads with unwholesome messages. First off, it was a headache, very nasty headache the boy had, but then he gets the voices, setting him on to murder his father.'

The finger finally arrived at the end of Elijah's nose.

'Arrest him! He'll bring down the plagues of Egypt upon us and we shall all be doomed!'

The Elders stood frozen, staring in horror at what Elijah had unleashed in their midst or, perhaps they thought, at a walking spirit. Elijah himself had come to the conclusion that William Senior was not so very dead after all, although it was possible that he believed himself to be.

The sergeant laid a pacifying hand upon his arm. 'Now then, Mr Aubrey, do calm down. This won't do. You aren't murdered, now, are you?'

William thought about it.

'Nah,' he said, finally, with a tinge of reluctance in his voice.

'You go and sit down, there's a good fellow, over there –' The sergeant pointed to a distant pew. William lowered the finger and set off more or less in the right direction. Elijah guessed that this must be a well-rehearsed procedure. The sergeant had probably been pacifying Aubreys since he was a probationary constable. He had most likely cut his teeth on William the First.

William having removed his bulk from between them, Elijah found that he was looking directly at the sergeant. The Elders were silent. Father had not moved or spoken since he had said good evening to the visitors. Elders

Foregate and Campion seemed to be losing all substance and colour, merging with the panelling behind them.

'Well, then,' the sergeant said encouragingly, 'let's have a look at this machine of yours with which you are alleged to have incited William Aubrey to murder his father William Aubrey. Come along, gentlemen. I take it you do possess this infernal machine.'

Elder Bland made a move. 'I can assure you, Sergeant, this is a house of God. None of us has committed any such offence. We are dedicated to peace and goodwill.'

There was a ripple of assent among the others, nods and shaken heads. Elijah perceived that they were subtly distancing themselves from him.

'My son has committed no crime,' Father said in a tremulous whisper. 'You cannot believe it.'

'Well, well, let's have a look at it, shall we?' the sergeant said, imperturbably. 'I suppose there *is* a machine?'

'Rays . . .' came distantly from the back of the hall.

'An apparatus,' Father said. 'Just an apparatus.'

'It's in here,' Elijah said, and led the way through the door.

The sergeant followed him into the committee room and walked over to the table, where he stood surveying the Electric Telepath. 'This is yours, is it?'

Father was at his elbow. 'There is no harm in it,' he said. 'We employ it solely to convey the still small voice to those who might otherwise fail to hear it. It is the voice of the Almighty as spoken to the prophet Elijah on Mount Horeb—'

'Yes, yes, I know all about that,' the sergeant said. He

gazed at the apparatus. 'Battery, one; terminals, two; Leyden jars, two; copper wire . . .' He turned and raised his eyebrows at Elijah. 'Isn't this what Oliver Lodge was using in 'eighty-seven?'

It seemed to Elijah that the room was suddenly flooded with light, as if from an arc lamp. The shadows fled away.

'I was trying to produce electromagnetic waves,' he said. 'I haven't got the equipment Hertz used, and I don't have a receiver—'

'But he excites the wave,' Father butted in. 'We've all seen it. And the receivers have, er, received.'

'Seen an electromagnetic wave?'

'They saw the spark,' Elijah said.

'And the waves carry the still small voice—'

Oh Dad, do shut up.

'Really? Well, now, sir, I don't believe they do,' the sergeant said. 'There's no telling what they may carry in the future, but at the present, all that's been conveyed by electromagnetic waves is Morse code, transmitted by Oliver Lodge, of whom I was speaking to your son, at Oxford, in August of this year. Perhaps one day they will carry sound, and perhaps the Good Lord will find a use for them, but I somehow doubt if your son has been putting murderous thoughts into people's heads by means of them.'

'You don't have to *put* murderous thoughts into the Aubreys' heads,' Elijah began.

'I'm aware of that,' the sergeant said, and managed to imply at the same time, *And I know what you've been up to*. 'Now, I think Mr Aubrey ought to look at this ray machine for himself. Just take the wires away, will you, we don't want to give him ideas – leave the jars. Mr Briggs, fetch Mr Aubrey, if you would be so good.'

When they were alone he turned to Elijah. 'What the devil have you been telling them? You know as well as I do—'

'I'm a member of the Congregation of Mount Horeb—'

'You could hardly be otherwise,' the sergeant said, 'but don't expect me to believe that you don't know exactly what you're doing. What is it you call this thing?'

Elijah deduced from his phrasing that the sergeant knew perfectly well what he called it.

'The Electric Telepath.'

'Telepathy's an interesting proposition and completely unproven.'

'I was doing electrical experiments in the book cupboard upstairs,' Elijah said. 'I couldn't find anywhere else. They then found all my apparatus; they'd have destroyed it, my father doesn't approve – I pretended it could be of use in our missions.'

'"How sharper than a serpent's tooth it is to have a thankless child,"' the sergeant said. '*King Lear*, by the poet Shakespeare.' He was cut short by the entry of William Senior with Elder Briggs. 'Are the jars charged?' he muttered.

Elijah nodded.

'Give him a spark, then.' He turned to William. 'Now, see here, Mr Aubrey, this is your machine.'

'Them pickle jars? Garn!'

'Send your wave,' the sergeant said, and Elijah discharged the jars. When he saw the spark William sighed with pleasure, as the Elders had done, but then looked disappointed.

'Is that it?'

''Fraid so,' the sergeant said. 'No rays, no unwholesome thoughts, just a wave of – of—' He noted William's look of incomprehension. 'Just a bit of electricity,' he ended lamely.

William gave an outraged snort. 'It's all flim-flam, ain't it? That Charlie Campion, coming round telling us to listen for the Word – and you!' He wheeled round to Elijah.

'No, I didn't,' Elijah said, relieved to be telling the truth for once. 'You volunteered, that first time.' He remembered the Aubreys were the last people he had wanted involved with the Electric Telepath.

'Ho, yes, the *first* time. Give this lot an inch and they'll take an ell,' William roared ungraciously. 'Never off your back, on an' on about the still small voice. And then they try and make out they can make us hear it even when we aren't listening, with them – them *gallipots*. It's a sell, that's what it is.'

Without turning his head to see the Elders clustered nervously round the doorway, the sergeant raised his voice to match William's bellow. 'I'm sorry to say that it *is* a sell, Mr Aubrey – not of course that there ever was any intention of selling it, *was there*? No suggestion of gaining *pecuniary advantage*. Now then, Mr Aubrey, let us go down to the station and collect your son, who is by now feeling thoroughly sorry—'

'So he should. He kicked me downstairs.'

'—feeling thoroughly sorry for himself, I was going to say. Of course, you may still wish to press charges for assault and battery.'

'Nah, I mean ter say,' William ruminated, 'after all, he *didn't* kill me. We'll make our peace.'

As they went out the sergeant turned to Elijah. 'And you, you young idiot, had better make peace with *your* father, and these others. I'm not sure what they were planning to do with your apparatus but word gets around, particularly when people like William are involved. Next time you get into a scrape, for God's sake tell the truth. If nothing else, it saves time.'

The sergeant and William Senior had departed. Elijah was left alone with the apparatus, miserably aware of the Elders on the far side of the door which the sergeant had closed behind him. On Elijah's side of the door stood his father.

The Old Man looked at him.

'Was it *all* untrue?' he said. 'Is the sergeant correct in what he says?' Elijah knew that he was praying to be told that the sergeant had been wrong and that Elijah had not deceived them. 'He seems to be an educated man.'

'He's right,' Elijah said. There was no point in pretending otherwise. 'I wasn't lying about the electromagnetic waves – and it's true about electricity, gas, magnetism – man hasn't invented them, we've only discovered them, discovered what we can do with them. We're still finding out. But the rest was a lie.'

Elder Briggs was imploring. 'Yet the sergeant said . . . Morse code has been transmitted by those waves. That perhaps one day . . .'

'Perhaps one day,' Elijah said. 'But not yet. Not now.'

'They will be so disappointed in Halifax.'

They will be disappointed much closer to home than Halifax, Elijah thought, looking at the door.

'They wanted to make money out of it,' he said, 'even though they knew it doesn't work.'

'Elder Brayfield didn't believe,' Father said. 'He tried to tell me but I wouldn't listen.'

'You couldn't believe I would lie to you.'

'No,' the Old Man said sadly. 'And you have taken the name of the Lord in vain.'

'I never meant to. But when Mrs Elligot found the equipment and the others were there, I was afraid you would make me destroy it.'

'No, I should not have done that,' Elder Briggs said slowly, 'but I should have told you to put it out of temptation's way until you had heard the still small voice. I suppose,' he said hopefully, 'you tired of waiting?'

Elijah could not, honestly, give him even that consolation.

'No, Father, I'm sorry. I do not believe I shall ever hear the still small voice. I believe I must decide for myself what becomes of me.'

Then he said the hardest thing of all.

'We have only one life. I must be the one who chooses what I shall do with mine.'

* * *

Afterwards he did not remember how he had left the chapel under the gaze of the Elders, but he hoped they were now gazing at each other – not at Father but at Campion and Foregate. Pecuniary advantage! What a splendid phrase. Surely the policeman had been sent to save him, to save them all.

Sent by whom? Why would anyone consider him worth saving?

He was walking down Cater Street, turning into Trimley Road, past the tram depot, and ahead of him Ryecart Road cut across. To the right lay the way home to number 57; to the left, number 216, where he had once imagined Paradise to be. Lily had known all along that the whole business of the Electric Telepath was nonsense, a sell. Flim-flam, William Senior had called it, and it had been on the verge of becoming something much worse. Could he not go to Lily now and say, 'We've been lying to one another. I knew it. You knew it. Can't we start again and tell the truth this time?'

While he thought about it he found that he was crossing the road and approaching the house on the corner of The Crescent. As he walked up the path he realized that he had neglected to check on the whereabouts of Mr Roper, but it was a safe bet that he was in his office, interviewing clients, making those ostentatious telephone calls, while his clerk inked in yet more squares and rectangles on the map.

And what was going to become of his own map, his work of art?

He rang the bell.

Work of art or not, he was fairly sure that next time he looked in at the chapel the map would have discreetly disappeared.

And what would become of the apparatus? How could he have left it there? Father had said that he would not have ordered it to be destroyed, but might not Bland or Brayfield, seeing it as Satan's tool, fall upon it; or Campion and Foregate, in thwarted rage—

On the other hand, they were probably afraid to touch it.

Someone was coming down the hall; he saw movement behind the yellow and red panes of the window in the door. Maggie opened it and stood there, gripping a Ewbank carpet sweeper by its handle, like one of the cherubim at the gates of Eden.

'Is Miss Roper at home?'

'No, she's not,' Maggie said, joyfully.

'Will she be – may I wait – I—'

'No she won't. No you may not.'

'I have to see her.' Why had he said that? But he did have to see her, urgently. Lily!

'Listen,' Maggie said, 'you may think you're welcome here but you're not. The only reason she puts up with you and your nonsense is because the Master, he said, and I heard him, "Lily, my girl, best keep in with that old fool Briggs and his God-bothering son. He could bring a lot of business my way." '

Elijah could only gape at her. Did camels smile? This must be how they must look.

'How could I bring him any business?'

'Not *you*,' Maggie crowed. 'Your dad; since he got on the council. Not that I was meant to tell *you*, but I gets great pleasure from doing so. Now, put that in your pipe and smoke it.'

She shut the door, leaving him in the porch, where he stood for more than a minute, digesting, if not smoking, what Maggie had told him.

Lily had been kidding him along, not for her own sake, or his, but on behalf of her father. Had the pompous old turkey-cock really believed he could gain pecuniary advantage by ingratiating himself at second hand with the incorruptible Joseph Briggs? His only consolation, if it could be called that, was that he had been quite as dishonest with her as she had been with him.

At least no one else had known.

Except Maggie.

And then, as he went to the gate, he saw three people coming down the road on the far side, from the direction of Holloway Hill. One of them was Gunnings, his old pal Gunnings, being a proper gentleman and walking on the outer edge of the pavement. Beside him was his sister, and arm-in-arm with the sister was Nonnie Gilstrap. Elijah felt himself turning to stone in the gateway.

Gunnings saw him and waved nonchalantly, but showed no signs of crossing over to speak to him. Elijah half waved, half raised his cap. Gunnings's sister and Nonnie instantly collapsed against each other in silent hysterics. Gunnings caught Elijah's eye, shrugged helplessly and walked on, leaving the girls to stagger in his wake.

At last Elijah managed to detach himself from the gate and walk away. He turned down The Crescent, skirted the brickworks and began to climb the hill across the frozen fields to where he had sat once before on the stile, to look down over the Trident. It seemed a good place to go and think things out, where no one was likely to pass him. What evil impulse had sent Honoria Gilstrap down Ryecart Road at the very moment that Maggie was expelling him from Eden?

Troubles come not as single spies, he thought. The poet Shakespeare again. But no one else had sent them. No one had sent the police sergeant to put an end to the Electric Telepath. The good and the bad alike simply happened; people made them happen. If anyone had come to the aid of the Horebites it was the God of the Horebites; he would have to find his own God.

The fog was creeping back across the Trident, and to the west, over Lembridge, the sun was sinking into it, a dull crimson sphere, its fires damped down for the night. In the old Greek tales Prometheus had stolen fire from heaven to light mankind, and the gods had punished him with eternal agony.

But hadn't Faraday taken fire from heaven to light mankind? And the sun had smiled upon his work and on all who came after him. No wonder pagans worshipped the sun.

He climbed over the stile and walked a little further up the hill to the fringe of the beech hanger to make the sunset last a little longer, and there he stood, to watch his god sinking into the twilight. All things were made by it, and without it was not anything made that was made.

DARKHENGE

Catherine Fisher

'Chloe?' he whispered.

The girl looked back. Her face was shadowed by great trees, their branches so low she had to duck under them. The sun shafted through forest.

He was sure. A narrow face, a smile like hers, not seen for three months. An impudent, spiteful smile. And a voice. It said, 'Hi, Robbie.'

Rob's sister Chloe lies in a coma after a riding accident, trapped in a forest of dreams between life and death. But when a dark druid shape-shifts his way into Rob's life, despair turns to hope. Because the druid knows the way through the Unworld, where he claims Chloe is imprisoned. Could the ominous black ring of timbers slowly emerging from a secret archaeological dig hold the key to rescuing her?

DEFINITIONS
0 370 32859 0

I CAPTURE THE CASTLE

Dodie Smith

This is the journal of Cassandra Mortmain; an extraordinary account of life with her equally extraordinary family. First, there is her eccentric father. Then there is her sister, Rose – beautiful, vain and bored – and her stepmother, Topaz, an artist's model who likes to commune with nature. Finally, there is Stephen, dazzlingly handsome and hopelessly in love with Cassandra.

In the cold and crumbling castle which is their home, Cassandra records events with characteristic honesty, as she tries to come to terms with her own feelings. The result is both marvellously funny and genuinely moving.

'This book has one of the most charismatic narrators I've ever met' *J.K. Rowling*

DEFINITIONS
0 09 984500 8

USEFUL IDIOTS

Jan Mark

A violent storm sweeps across Parizo beach and unveils a human skull beneath the sands. It has much to reveal about the past . . .

In the year 2255, the British Isles have altered beyond recognition. The world's climate has changed and rising seas have engulfed the east of the islands. In what is left of the land, an Aboriginal community, the Inglish, cling to an archaic way of life. They claim the skull as one of their own.

Merrick, a young graduate in the 'lost' science of archaeology, finds that his interest in the remains draws him into a cultural struggle he doesn't understand. His claustrophobic involvement with the Inglish leads him to become a willing guinea pig in a bizarre and painful experiment in evolution.

'Brimming with ideas . . . a book with great ambition' *Guardian*

'Unforgettable. . . A thriller that grabs you by the throat and doesn't let go until the end' *TES*

DEFINITIONS
0 099 4730 0

THE SHELL HOUSE

Linda Newbery

When Greg stumbles across the beautiful ruins of Graveney Hall, he becomes intrigued by the story behind its destruction. He and his friend Faith are drawn into a quest to discover the fate of Graveney's last heir, Edmund, a young soldier who disappeared in mysterious circumstances during the First World War.

But Greg's investigations force him to question his own views on love and faith, and reveal more about himself than he would ever have imagined.

A beautiful portrayal of love, sexuality and spirituality over two generations.

SHORTLISTED FOR THE GUARDIAN CHILDREN'S FICTION PRIZE

'Intelligent and perceptive' *Guardian*

'Newbery writes wonderfully' *Financial Times*

'This is a novel to read, think about, and then read again' *Independent*

DEFINITIONS
0 09 945593 5